# The Keeper of the Western Door

# The Keeper of the Western Door

CARLA KELLY

Interior Design by Cora Johnson
Edited by Haley Swan and Lisa Shepherd
Cover design by Rachael Anderson and Kennedy Anderson
Cover Photo Credits:
Period Images: Mary Chronis VJ Dunraven Productions
Deposit Photos: Zrfphoto 210858672
Symbol: Seneca Nation

Published by Mirror Press, LLC
ISBN: 978-1-952611-51-3

*This story was originally published in the Timeless Western Collection: Calico Ball*

## Other Works by Carla Kelly

A Naval Surgeon to Fight For
The Lady's Companion
Regency Glad Tidings
The Wedding Journey
Libby's London Merchant
One Good Turn
Where Dreams Meet
Her Smile
My Loving Vigil Keeping
The Unlikely Master Genius
The Unlikely Spy Catchers
The Unlikely Heroes
The Unlikely Gun Warf Rats
Calico Ball
A Wyoming Summer

*In memory of Henrietta Blueye,*
*who once told me that every girl should have*
*the Radcliffe experience.*

"Remember that some of the greatest needs
may be those right in front of you."

Bonnie Oscarson
October 2017

# Prologue

Blame it on Mrs. O'Leary's cow, although the jury is still out on the matter, and the cow wasn't talking. On October 8, 1871, around nine o'clock at night, the unnamed cow kicked over a lantern in the O'Leary's barn, located on DeKoven Street in Chicago, Illinois.

The fire spread rapidly through the mostly wooden city, dry from summer drought. After two days and nights, the flames wore themselves out, moving north and helped along by rain. Three hundred people died, with 17,500 buildings burned and 100,000 rendered homeless.

News of the disaster reached Fort Laramie, Wyoming Territory, via a telegram, which was admittedly brief. Since the Union

Pacific Railroad now passed through Cheyenne, 110 miles south, more detailed newspapers made their way to the fort when troopers rode south for mail and supplies.

"My word, Chicago is suffering," Mrs. Gertrude Hayes told her husband over breakfast on Officers' Row one morning in mid October.

She handed the paper to Captain Hayes, G Troop, Fifth Cavalry. He read it with his porridge. Oatmeal was his least favorite breakfast, but that was the army. There was a current overabundance of oats and raisins in the commissary. Too bad there was never a surplus of eggs.

When Captain Hayes left for guard mount, Mrs. Hayes began to wonder what to do for Chicago. She knew the city well enough, with its rows of wooden houses, most with shingled or tarred roofs. A woman of some imagination, Gertrude Hayes could picture desperate women fleeing with babes in arms and little more. Newspaper in hand, she walked next door to the post surgeon's quarters, where she found Mrs. Stanley staring at *her* newspaper.

Gertrude plunked herself down. They were friends of great standing, having moved together from garrison to garrison since before the War of the Rebellion. "Augusta, how can we help these pitiful folk?" she asked.

Augusta Stanley was cut from the same army cloth. "Let's have fun and do some good at the same time. We should hold a calico ball."

"I've heard of them," Mrs. Hayes said. "Heavens, who hasn't?"

"Granted, we are pretty small potatoes out here," Augusta Stanley said (she was regrettably prone to slang). "If every lady made a calico dress and wore it, we could send the dresses to the poor women in Chicago. We should include the sergeants' wives in this ball."

"Would we charge the men one dollar admission?" Mrs. Hayes asked.

"At least. We can donate refreshments. The regimental band will play."

The women looked at each other, thoughtful, because the next matter loomed. Neither was prone to much exertion, and rank did have its privileges.

"Who should be in charge of this event?"

"Who is the lowest-ranking lieutenant in the garrison?" Mrs. Stanley asked.

"Lieutenant Yeatman, I Company, and a bachelor. He won't do."

As the sound of the band faded away, indicating the end of guard mount, Mrs. Stanley and Mrs. Hayes thought a little more.

"I have it," Mrs. Hayes declared. "Lieutenant Masterson's wife. He is my husband's brand new second lieutenant. I'll grant you Victoria Masterson is self-centered, but she has what we need."

"Come again?"

"Augusta, think a moment. Can *you* sew a dress?"

"Certainly not. That is what the lower orders are for."

"Precisely," Mrs. Hayes said. "Victoria Masterson's maid—you know, the one with the silly name—is a seamstress without equal. She sews all of Victoria's clothing, and you know smart *she* always looks."

"Yes, Mary Blue Eye," Mrs. Stanley said. "My husband says that is a Seneca or Mohawk name. But will she do it?"

"Of course! It's time Victoria Masterson learned how things are done in the army. The Blue Eye maid has no choice."

# ONE

MARY BLUE EYE was no snob. It was an unlikely title for someone serving as a maid to a friend. To be honest, maybe less of a friend than Mary had thought last summer, when she grudgingly agreed to accompany newly married Victoria Masterson from New York to Fort Laramie.

Yet here she stood in front of the dining room mirror, staring at a woman sort of tan, with dark hair and eyes. True, she was Seneca, but far superior to the luckless Sioux and Cheyenne lurking around Fort Laramie, begging for handouts. Wasn't she?

Sergeant Blade was the only person in the entire garrison who might understand her growing doubts, but he wasn't available for idle chat. She didn't even know his first name. She couldn't ask Victoria's husband, Lieutenant Silas Masterson, if he could send G Troop's first sergeant over for cookies and milk when there was nothing better to do.

The best Mary could hope for was to run into him in the sutler's store, which so far hadn't happened. She did enjoy watching the sergeant lead new recruits through the mysteries of equitation on the parade ground. He had a brisk air of command that brooked no disobedience from man or beast. He was also not a man to idle away his time anywhere appropriate for Mary to meet him.

Not that she ever wanted to recreate the one time when she had him all to herself, albeit briefly. They were a day out of Cheyenne, traveling to Fort Laramie in an army ambulance, which amused Victoria Masterson until she realized it was the common mode of transportation for army dependents, and not as comfortable as her father's carriage back home.

They had bumped along over nasty trails, mashed together in the ambulance with the wife of G Troop's first lieutenant and their three children, the wife growing more irritated with each mile that her darlings were crowded tighter than clams in a basket.

Ignoring Mary, the woman finally addressed Victoria. "Mrs. Masterson, tell your maid to ride with the baggage so Anthony can stretch out before he pukes."

Startled, Victoria had nudged Mary. "Would you mind?"

"*Mind?* Mrs. Masterson, she is your servant," the woman said. "Tell her."

Victoria spoke to the driver through the canvas barrier. He stopped his horses, and Mary got out without a word, humiliated.

Sergeant Blade had been riding beside the ambulance. He dismounted and asked what the problem was.

"Where's the baggage wagon?" Mary asked. "Not enough room in here for me."

"Lieutenant Caldwell's wife is not known for tact," he said as he walked her to a blue-painted wagon with red wheels. "Let me help you up."

The help-up meant hands on her waist and a boost that landed her beside the driver, who saluted the sergeant with a casual two fingers to his cap. "I'll look after her, Sarge."

"See that you do," Sergeant Blade said. Coming out of *his* mouth, it was no suggestion.

That was that, almost. The sergeant mounted and rode beside the wagon, pacing his horse. "I'm afraid you have to eat dust back here. I'll see what I can do."

When she didn't say anything because she was too embarrassed, he side stepped his mount closer to the wagon. "May I help you?" he asked.

She saw so much concern on his face. She knew there was nothing he could do, but he was kind to say it, and so she told him. He nodded.

"You're not used to being a maid, are you?"

"No, sir," she said, not sure how to address a sergeant. "I thought I was a friend."

She looked away so he wouldn't see her tears, and he rode to the top of the detail after one backward glance. It was then that she understood something about the army—sergeants were in charge of everyone in the command. The knowledge warmed her heart and made the dust almost bearable.

They had camped that night beside the Chugwater. Lieutenant Caldwell's wife had included a cook in her entourage, so the Mastersons fared well enough. Unsure of herself, Mary stood close to Victoria.

"Should I take a plate?" Mary whispered.

"I don't know," her childhood friend whispered back. "I don't see any of the other servants eating here."

*I'm hungry, too*, Mary thought. She looked around until she saw another woman who had been riding in the other baggage wagon. Nothing ventured, nothing gained.

She walked to the other campfire and waited there, not sure what to do. The woman glanced at her briefly, then glanced away, hunching her shoulder as if she didn't want to know her.

Startled, Mary walked away. If she could find a water barrel, at least there would be something to drink. She remembered longhouse elders smoking their pipes and talking about starvation marches as they fought with the British against the American colonists.

*I should have brought along some pemmican, except I can't stand pemmican*, she thought, which made her smile. *I'm a pretty poor Seneca.*

She found a water barrel with a tin cup beside it and dipped herself a drink. She relished the coolness, even though the water tasted of wood, with just a hint of tar, probably from the lining. She rolled it around in her mouth, thinking of Papa and his favorite brandy, an annual Christmas gift from Victoria's father, Judge Wilkins.

"I can offer you something better," she heard behind her, and knew she was about to be cared for.

Sergeant Blade held out a tin plate with what looked like smashed hardtack. She took the plate, her mouth watering from the bacon that the mangled crackers were cooked in.

He handed her a fork and indicated a log. She sat down and he joined her. Too shy to speak and hungry, she ate in silence, relishing the odd combination.

"Why does this taste so good?" she asked, knowing about manners and conversation, and after all, he had found her a meal.

"One of two things," he said. "You're either really hungry, or food cooked over a buffalo chip fire is well . . . uh . . . seasoned."

She laughed out loud. "Doesn't even need pepper."

"Good to hear you laugh," Sergeant Blade said. "You were looking pretty glum earlier." He was silent for a moment, then, "And I don't blame you."

Her stomach was full. She wasn't thirsty. The sky had darkened, and Mary felt bold enough to ask the man seated beside her something that had been bothering her since she and Victoria Masterson had seen their first Indians in Nebraska.

"Sir, do I look like an Indian?"

She asked it quietly, partly because it seemed like a frivolous question, and partly because she doubted she should even mention the matter.

"Everyone calls me Sarge," he told her. "You can too."

"Very well." Maybe he wasn't going to answer her question.

"Yes, you do," he said, "but you don't. Tell me more."

"Are you certain?" she asked, doubtful. Maybe it was time for her to return to the ambulance and see if Victoria needed her for anything. But that would mean walking past the other servant who had turned away, and facing the lieutenant's wife again.

"I'm interested. I've never met an eastern Indian, if that's what you are."

"I am Seneca," she told him. "My family is descended from Mary Jemison, a captive who chose to stay with the Keepers of the Western Door. Her second husband was Hiakatoo, a Seneca. Their daughter Jane is my grandmother. We live in a nice house on property belonging to Victo . . . Mrs. Masterson's father, Judge Wilkins. My mother is his cook, and my father is the judge's secretary. We're Methodists." *So maybe I am not much of an Indian*, she thought.

"If I'm not being rude, do most Seneca look like you?" he asked.

"Some do, some don't," she said, hearing nothing in his question but curiosity. "There's been some marrying back and forth." She looked toward the other campfire. "I suppose I had better go over there."

"Do you want to?"

That was precisely what she had been asking herself ever since she was evicted from the officers' ambulance. She glanced at Sergeant Blade and again saw nothing but goodwill in his expression.

"Part of me does, and part of me doesn't," she said, which made him chuckle. "I don't think I belong in the West, but I promised Mrs. Masterson I would stay for six months, and so I shall. Goodnight, Sergeant."

She didn't ask, but he walked her back to the officers' campfire. "I'll tell the teamster to shift around some boxes in the baggage wagon," he said as they came closer. "Throw your bedroll in there. You'll be safe, and I won't worry."

"Why would you worry at all?"

"You're part of my job, and I like you," he said simply. "Good night, Miss Blue Eye. Things will go better tomorrow."

# TWO

THEY DIDN'T, EXCEPT that Mary learned something about herself on that last day's travel to Fort Laramie. She also learned more about Sergeant Blade.

She had resumed her place in the baggage wagon, seated this time on the open tailgate because it was cooler. To console herself, Mary indulged in a hearty round of self-pity, wondering how soon she could leave. Mama had sent her West with enough money for a return ticket.

Here she was now, hanging on for dear life to the chain that lowered the gate. Mary hadn't dangled her feet over the edge of anything in years. She was happy to face away from trail dust and breathe better air.

She hung on tighter when the wagon began its descent into what was probably a reluctant creek that had been emboldened by a recent series of gully-washing rains. Muddy water swirled around the wheels, and two things happened at once.

The nearest crate slid off the end of the wagon and pulled her with it, plopping into the water and sucking her down. Frantic, she tried to scream and ended up gargling mud. She bloodied her fingers, feeling for a hold on the rough wood of the crate, then forcing her fingers through a small opening.

Trouble was, the crate held china—she felt sodden newspaper and ceramic—and began to sink as it bumped along. She turned her attention to worming her fingers out of the slat, ready to strike out for the bank. The weight of her dress wore her down, too. Her shoes were already gone, which helped, but the dress was heavy.

She shrieked when a horse blocked her view, then realized salvation loomed. She yanked her hand free and held it up, to be grasped by Sergeant Blade, who leaned down and grabbed whatever else was handy, which turned out to be her shirtwaist. With no ceremony, he threw her stomach-down over his lap and transferred his spare hand to the back of her skirt, working his gauntleted hand into her waistband.

"Hang on."

*To what?* she asked herself, then grabbed his leg, which he obligingly raised a little so she could put her forearm between his thigh and the saddle.

"Damned steep bank," he muttered, then up they went, after crossing the swollen stream and charging up the other side.

Safe now, she let him gently lower her to the ground, her sodden dress and petticoats sticking to her, and the buttons gone from her shirtwaist where he had grabbed her. She didn't care. She was alive.

She covered her face with her hands. Perhaps it was vestigial memory—heaven knows the Seneca had little to fear recently except prejudice—but her mother had taught her never to cry in times of struggle, never to invite unwelcome sound into any fraught situation. She stood there in silence, alone until Sergeant Blade dismounted and pulled her close.

"You all right?" he asked.

She nodded, not all right a bit and wanting her mother in the worst way.

"Liar," he said, which made her laugh, too. Maybe she *was* all right.

Victoria Masterson came running, but not too fast, because she was a lady, and not too close, because of all the mud.

Then Sergeant Blade astounded Mary, amazed her, and warmed her heart to a profound degree. "Mrs. Masterson, Miss Blue Eye leaped into the water to save your china."

Two thoughts seemed to collide inside Victoria Masterson's admittedly roomy brain: Her china was gone. Her servant-friend had risked her life for it.

Victoria gasped and started to cry. She didn't go so far as to embrace her soaking wet servant, but she held out her hand. "Thank you, Mary," she said. "I'll never forget this."

*Yes, you will,* Mary thought, even as she wanted to laugh at the sergeant's adroit interpretation of the event. *And you, Sarge, should be a diplomatist.*

"Do you have dry clothes in the baggage wagon?" Sergeant Blade asked.

Mary nodded, her face warm because it was a delicate subject. He helped her into the wagon, told the driver to back away, and organized a few troopers to travel downstream to see what they could salvage from the crate, if anything.

Dry except for her hair and at least partly clean, Mary took a seat beside the driver, who looked at her with some awe now as the selfless attempted rescuer of a doomed china crate. She watched Sergeant Blade ride to the head of the column beside his officers, touched in her heart that his artless lie had made her a heroine and smoothed a path.

She was certain the army didn't pay him enough.

# Three

But how did a body find an opportunity to get to know such a man better? Mary still stood before the mirror, which was not getting any silver polished. She sat down at the dining room table and applied herself to tarnish.

It wasn't a dining room. Second lieutenants were entitled to four rooms, if available, and none were. The Mastersons had crammed the table into a corner of the tiny parlor. Victoria had made quite a show of insisting that they call this side the dining room and the other side the parlor.

Mary knew better than to argue. She had known Victoria all her life, well aware that once she dug in with an idea, it was there to stay, no matter how ridiculous. A new husband, Silas hadn't learned his lesson yet. Mary had to pretend she didn't hear a spirited argument that night. By morning, he was calling that corner of the room the dining room, and peace reigned.

Mary's room was a curtained alcove off the kitchen, probably meant for a cook. Once a bed had been crammed into the small space, there was room for little else.

A cook. Another lively fight involved a question from the lieutenant, sounding both aggrieved and aghast: "You can't cook *anything*?" At least, that was all Mary heard before he slammed the bedroom door.

The Mastersons had solved that thorny issue by hiring a corporal's wife from G Troop who claimed she could cook. The wary woman appeared for dinner, but took Mary aside to give her a shake and order her to manage breakfast and luncheon for Mrs. High-and-Mighty. "Boil eggs and make biscuits," she snapped, then made it worse. "Even an Indian can do that."

Mary had set the last of the spoons in warm water when Victoria Masterson came home, quite the reverse of the confident woman earlier, answering a summons from the company commander's and post surgeon's wives, acknowledged leaders of Fort Laramie's elite, at least according to them.

The lady of the house sank into a chair and stared at the dishpan holding her spoons. Mary waited, confident that her friend/employer/who knew? would eventually speak.

A massive sigh came first, followed by the drama. "I do not know what I have got myself into," she said.

Mary remained silent. Her mother had taught her the virtue of silence when dealing with "those of lighter skin," as Mama put it. She waited.

"Or rather, what two perfectly capable women have got me into," Victoria amended, and glared at Mary, probably because she was handy.

Silence still seemed wise to Mary.

"Mary, have you heard of a calico ball?"

Mary thought of an excruciating time ten years ago when she was eleven and her tribe had suffered through a poor harvest, followed by diphtheria. The Blue Eye family had been largely immune, since they lived on Judge Wilkins's property, away from contagion.

"Yes, I have," she said. "Remember that bad winter when so many babies died?"

Victoria shook her head, which came as no surprise to Mary.

"Some of the ladies in the First Presbyterian Church held a calico ball, with proceeds and dresses going to my people," Mary told her. Mama had politely handed back the dress Victoria's own mother thought to give her, after the ball. She didn't need it. When Mrs. Masterson insisted, Mama cut it down for Mary, who didn't need it either.

"I remember now. That was so kind of the church ladies," Victoria said. Another sigh, then, "Mrs. Hayes and Mrs. Stanley are organizing a calico ball, with dresses and proceeds for the poor of Chicago, who lost everything in that fire."

Mary had a sudden vision of thousands of poor ladies lined up for perhaps twenty dresses headed their way from a four-company garrison in the middle of nowhere.

"It might be a worthy project," she said cautiously.

"*Might* be," Victoria said, with barely controlled distress. "Who is put in charge but the wife of the lowest-ranking officer on post? Me!"

"Hmm," seemed like the wisest reply.

Then came The Look, which Mary recognized. She steeled herself.

"I assured those two biddies that I have the perfect solution to calico dresses on demand. Surely you can guess."

"No, I can't." Mary said. Dread began to loom over her shoulder like a perched vulture.

"You can make the dresses!"

Mary stared at her employer and perhaps by this time, former friend. "But . . . With only a needle and thread? Victoria, I . . ."

"Better call me Mrs. Masterson. I know it seems so formal, but you do work for me now," Victoria said. "Mrs. Stanley has already corrected me about that."

Definitely former friend. Thank goodness the Union Pacific ran both west *and* east throughout the coming winter. "How many dresses?"

"Perhaps fifteen. That would take care of the officers' wives, who, I scarcely need tell you, don't sew." She laughed. "Don't look so stunned! Heaven knows why, but Mrs. Hayes has a sewing machine. You have plenty of time. The dance is in four weeks."

Four weeks. Mrs. Masterson obviously had no idea how long fifteen dresses would take. "And my other duties?"

"Oh, pish posh. You'll have time." Victoria looked at the clock. "Let's go to the sutler's store and look over the calico."

*After which I will run away*, Mary thought. Too bad Fort Laramie was surrounded by hostiles who wouldn't stop to politely inquire if she had any Indian blood before scalping her.

The sutler's supply of calico proved to be nonexistent. Mary watched Victoria stand in front of the dry goods counter and stare, as if hoping that bolts of fabric would suddenly—poof!—materialize. Alas, no.

Next stop was Mrs. Hayes's quarters,

where Victoria gave the captain's wife the sad news.

Mrs. Hayes took it in true army stride. "Simple. We'll send uh—Mary, is it?—Mary to Cheyenne with a cavalry troop in a day or two. She can pick out fabric, hurry back here, and start sewing."

Mary knew better than to look around. *Am I invisible? Can you ask me?* she thought.

"I should go, too," Victoria said.

"Heavens no, my dear! Hostiles are out and about. It would never do if something happened to you," Mrs. Hayes said. "Mary can go."

Mary realized two things: first, she was expendable; second, perhaps Mama and Papa shouldn't have spoiled her so much, going so far as to assure her that she was as good as a white woman. Maybe there was a third matter. In the eyes of these people, Victoria Masterson included now, she was an Indian servant in a place with no use for Indians.

# FOUR

THE WALK BACK to the Mastersons' quarters featured nothing beyond the crunch of shoes on gravel, Victoria well beyond her usual languid stroll. Indecisive, she stood in the tiny alcove they laughingly called a foyer. Her mind made up, she mashed her hat down more firmly.

"Start luncheon, Mary. I'm going to find Lieutenant Masterson."

Mary warmed the soup and buttered the bread. When they first arrived at Fort Laramie, the two of them had sat down together for lunch and chatted. That ended after Mrs. Stanley popped in unannounced one day and found them sitting together.

Almost, but not quite, in a whisper, Mrs.

Stanley set the new bride straight as Mary listened from the kitchen, hearing enough words to be chastised, which was probably the entire intention of the surgeon's wife: "Not done . . . she's your servant . . . remember her place . . ." Mary heard the unkind words long after Mrs. Stanley flounced away.

Mary ate in the kitchen, then went onto the porch to watch for Victoria. "I could have told you, had you asked me, that it's bad form to go traipsing after your husband in a garrison," Mary said under her breath.

She sat in a rocking chair and indulged in her favorite fantasy of imagining herself aboard an eastbound train. She heard a small noise and glanced over the railing to see an Indian woman with a little girl and a baby on her back. Mary had noticed them last week at the slaughtering floor behind the commissary storehouse. Some of the more bedraggled women stood there during the slaughter, begging silently with their eyes for whatever the army didn't want.

Victoria had sent her to the storehouse for another pound or two of the endless raisins that some harried clerk had sent their way from Omaha, perhaps mistaking an order of one hundred pounds for one thousand, which meant enough raisins to see them into the twentieth century.

The private in Fort Laramie's storehouse was equally harried and insisted that she needed ten pounds instead of the more modest two that Victoria had requested. "I don't care what you do with them," he said, then gestured toward the slaughterhouse. "Find some Indians." His face grew solemn. "They're always hungry."

Mary had done precisely that. She stopped a woman carrying a bloody bucket of entrails and brains and handed her small daughter a brown paper parcel bunched together and tied with twine. Gesturing with her fingers to her mouth, the universal sign for food that Mary knew from back home, she took some loose raisins from her basket and held them out.

After a glance toward her mother, who nodded, the little one popped the raisins in her mouth, chewed, and smiled. She was a pretty child, with snapping brown eyes and hair neatly bound into two braids.

Here they were again, standing silently at the edge of the porch, looking hopeful. They must have watched her return to this house last week, after she left the storehouse. Gesturing that they come closer, Mary hurried inside to the kitchen and poured more raisins into parcel paper.

She opened the side door and gave the raisins to the child, receiving smiles in return, ample payment. Mary watched them walk toward the slaughter yard again. She noted the child's ragged dress and wondered if the poor women of Chicago were better off, even with half of their city burned. Mama had told her more than once that charity begins at home.

She walked around to the porch to see Sergeant Blade standing there, looking where she had looked.

"They don't have much, do they?" he commented. "The clerk in the storehouse told me last week that he was liberal with raisins, and you were, too."

"I hope that won't get me thrown in the guardhouse," Mary said, not certain if levity was the better part of valor, concerning a sergeant.

"No. I expect a lot of us would like to help," he said, and followed her onto the porch. "I know I would."

"Can't you?" she asked, curious.

"That's a problem with being a first sergeant, Miss Blue Eye. We're supposed to follow all regulations. Even stupid ones," he said. "I'll leave the charity to you."

What did one do with a sergeant on the porch? Mary knew she couldn't ask him inside; it wasn't her house, and no one was home. He solved her problem by indicating the rocking chair while he perched on the porch railing, somehow managing to look dignified while doing it. She decided this was not a man bothered much by inconvenience.

"I'm here to warn you," he began, with no preliminaries other than a glance over his shoulder toward the parade ground. "You are going to Cheyenne for calico."

"Apparently your captain's wife told Mrs. Masterson that the trip was too dangerous for her, but not for me," Mary said. She wished she could hide the edge to her voice. "After all, we must have calico."

"You *will* be all right. I guarantee it. I'm leading the patrol. We are also to escort the paymaster, who is arriving tomorrow from Fort Fetterman, on his way to the railroad in Cheyenne."

He stood up and didn't disguise the edge to *his* voice. "He wants the ambulance to himself." She saw the discomfort on his face. "That's partly my doing. I asked if a lady could share it with him. He asked who she was, and I . . ."

". . . told him Miss Blue Eye, whereupon Major Pettifog decided it was a small ambulance and couldn't possibly accommodate another person," Mary finished.

"Bravo, Miss Blue Eye!" Sergeant Blade exclaimed. "Major Pettifog, indeed. Actually, his name is Pettigrew, so you were close."

"And he doesn't much care for Indians." Mary said what she knew he would not say. "I've heard it before."

"Even back East?"

"Not as much there. My skin is light, and I tend to blend in." She looked at the woman and child in the distance now. "Not so much out here."

"No, and more's the pity." He waved his hand. "Change of subject. Can you ride horseback?"

Mary couldn't help her smile. "I've been riding since I was young. I brought my riding skirt along, but I don't have a sidesaddle."

"I'll find you one. It'll be a fast trip. Major Pettigrew is eager to return to the comforts of Omaha. I am also informed by an unimpeachable source that there are many dresses for you to sew."

"Please don't tell me that Mrs. Masterson made a scene, with tears and demands," she blurted out.

"I won't, then," the sergeant said, amused. "Suffice it to say we all heard a convincing argument for calico."

Mary sighed.

"How did you get involved in this nonsense? It couldn't have been your idea."

She looked over his shoulder to see the Mastersons walking across the parade ground now. "Here they come. I will blame Mrs. O'Leary's cow back in Chicago. Think of the abuse that poor bovine will suffer in coming years."

The sergeant chuckled at that. "Tell me quick, because I want to know."

"Mrs. Masterson was put in charge of a calico ball because she is married to a second lieutenant who only outranks earthworms."

Aware the Mastersons were advancing, he laughed silently. "You are wise beyond your years, Miss Blue Eye. I suppose you can sew and she cannot, and you've suddenly become responsible for a lot of dressmaking because other ladies are equally helpless."

"Precisely, Sergeant."

"My name is Rowan."

"I'm Mary."

"Ready to ride the day after tomorrow?"

"As I'll ever be."

He gave her a small salute that made her smile. There was something in his eyes that reminded her of her own father, although they looked nothing alike. Maybe it was his genuine interest, which she knew she did not merit, because he barely knew her. She could probably tell him anything.

"Sergea . . . Rowan," she began.

He inclined his head in her direction, an invitation to continue.

"I think . . . I wish we could make dresses for that Indian woman and her little girl who are right here at Fort Laramie," she said. "I don't think they've rubbed up against much good luck lately if they're carrying buckets of guts."

"They haven't," Rowan agreed. "Over the Laramie beyond Suds Row, there's a whole camp of them that get by on handouts. Maybe her man died in a buffalo hunt. Maybe disease took him. They're on their own. Some people call them Laramie Loafers, but they work so hard to stay alive." He clapped his hands together, and she saw his frustration. "The West is changing, Mary Blue Eye. It's not a kind place for people who used to be the lords of the earth."

"I can understand that," she replied. "I'll be ready. Really early?"

"Really early."

# FIVE

TWO DAYS LATER, with a pouch of money from ladies needing dresses, Mary found herself thrown into the saddle by a man who knew what he was doing. She smiled down at the sergeant, pleased to be riding with a well-organized, efficient troop, and not negotiating life, for a few days at least, with a childish employer and her increasingly baffled husband.

*I am with an adult*, she thought, relieved and not a little amused. "Just tell me what to do, and I will do it," she told Sergeant Blade. "I mean, I can stay out of the way however is most convenient."

"All you have to do is ride beside me. No

eating dust on *this* trip. I'll take better care of you."

Why should that make her face go warm? The perpetual wind blowing cool across her face helped tamp down the pink. Thank goodness the sergeant had turned away to speak to Major Pettigrew, department paymaster who had finished his circuit of forts and was headed to headquarters in Omaha.

He turned back, and she noted that his face was red, too. Perhaps the wind was stronger than she thought. Or perhaps he wasn't any more practiced in female conversation than she was with talking to men not of her family. Mama had been scrupulous about her only daughter's deportment.

"Miss Blue Eye," he began more formally. She doubted the sergeant had mentioned to his troops that he was already calling her Mary.

"Yes, Sergeant?" she asked, not slow by any means.

She saw the appreciation in his eyes. "Major Pettigrew here has suggested you put the calico fabric money in the strongbox as we travel to the railroad."

She leaned over and handed the pouch to the major. "That way I won't be tempted to steal it, will I?"

"Miss Blue Eye, I didn't mean . . ."

"Sergeant, I know *you* didn't," she said, wondering where her nerve was coming from. "Major Pettigrew will feel safer if an Indian doesn't carry it."

"*You're* the Indian?" the paymaster said as he took the money.

"I am, sir," Mary said.

"I wouldn't have known," he replied. "I thought . . ."

"I know," she said, and started backing up her horse to get out of the conversation. "We Easterners of the Iroquois League do tend to look lighter, don't we? But I understand your reluctance." She couldn't help but notice admiration in Sergeant Blade's eyes. Whether it was the expert way she handled her mount or the fact that she stood up for herself, Mary had no idea. "I am Seneca, from Genesee, New York. My great-grandmother was Mary Jemison, whom you have perhaps heard of."

The major nodded. "Anyone who has read any history at all has heard of Mary Jemison."

What had gotten into her? "I am named for her. My great-grandfather was Hiakatoo, Mary's second husband. And imagine this: my father is a graduate of Dartmouth College."

The major tried to return the pouch, but Mary backed her horse farther away. "No. It is safer with you, sir. I trust every man in this detail, but who knows who we will run into? I trust you, too," she added, feeling generous.

Mary sat a little straighter, overwhelmed by what she had just done. Up to this moment, she had spent much of her life hoping no one would notice that she was different from Victoria Masterson's other friends, or that she knew how to ride, or sit quietly in council in the longhouse. *I am Seneca*, she thought, *I am a Keeper of the Western Door*. She would have to write to Papa and let him know. It was a letter long overdue.

She sat quietly by herself as Sergeant Blade continued his work. When the detail had lined up, he motioned her closer, and she obliged.

They left the fort's corral area as the sun rose, fanning out soon so no one had to eat dust. Sergeant Blade set a brisk pace.

Mary knew she had said too much to Major Pettigrew. He probably meant well.

"Should I apologize to Major Pettigrew?" she asked her riding companion.

"Under no circumstances," Rowan said, with no hesitation. "I don't mind that he feels a little downtrodden." He looked around at his troopers. "You have a lot of allies here." He laughed, mostly to himself. "After all, they remember how you so selflessly leaped into the water to save Mrs. Masterson's china."

She shook her head at that one. "Sergeant Bl—"

"Rowan."

"Very well then, Rowan! You're fighting my battles, and I don't know why."

"It feels good," he said, after a lengthy pause worthy of a Seneca elder.

They rode in silence for some distance. It

was enough to pound along on a good horse and breathe deep of autumn advancing and winter coming. There was something beguiling about the expanse of earth and sky here that appealed to her. No wonder the admittedly more primitive Sioux and Cheyenne were reluctant to give it up and submit tamely to a reservation. She understood. There were old Seneca who wore sad faces when they talked about land no longer theirs.

Mary watched the sergeant and saw his head on a nearly continuous swivel, watching, always watching. When they reached an area where the terrain became more gullied, he motioned to a rider on each end of the fan. When they rode ahead, the other soldiers pulled back into a double file.

"We're in an area where Sioux don't mind lying in wait to cause a bit of trouble," he told Mary. "If I see warriors, I'm plunking you in the ambulance."

She nodded and sidled her mount closer to his, an act that wasn't lost on the sergeant.

"You'll be fine, Mary," he said. "In fact,

talk to me. Do you live on a reservation? I don't know anything about the Seneca."

Silently, she blessed the man beside her. She knew he was keeping her calm by letting her talk.

"My family lives on land that used to belong to Mary Jemison herself."

"The White Indian of the Genesee," Sergeant Blade said. "I'm from Connecticut, and I remember hearing the stories."

She thought she had heard a bit of New England in Rowan Blade's speech. "I am named after her: Mary Jemison Blue Eye." She couldn't help her sigh. "Everyone back home calls me Jemmy. Mrs. Masterson used to."

"What do you like to be called?"

No one had ever asked her that before. "I'm used to Jemmy."

"May I continue to call you Mary? *I* like it."

She wanted to tell the tall, careful man riding beside her that Mary would be a name for no one but him and her. Her practical nature reined in that thought. *He's just making conversation,* she told herself, but yes, she would be Mary now to this man.

"Certainly you may," she said, keeping her voice low. "I like it, too."

She wanted to say more, but the point rider on the west rode toward Sergeant Blade, who spurred his mount ahead. She looked around and noticed that all of the troopers watched intently, some leaning forward, ready to do immediate bidding. The corporal edged his horse closer to hers.

"Sarge's orders, ma'am," he said cheerfully. "If he's not beside you, I am."

"Is he this careful with all his hangers-on?" she joked, and the corporal surprised her.

"Nope. Just you."

"All because I tried to rescue a crate of china a few months ago?" she asked.

"He didn't mention any china, ma'am," the corporal replied, and there was no overlooking the twinkle in his eyes. "Here he is. Sarge?"

Rowan motioned his men to gather closer. When Mary started to back off, he reached for her reins and kept her there.

"Private Reilly saw a handful of chipper fellows in the next draw," he said. "No one's painted up, though. Be alert but not overly interested. Maybe they're just playing mumblety-peg."

The troopers chuckled at that. Mary saw no fear. "Where do you want me?" she asked.

"In the ambulance," Rowan said. He tightened his grip on her reins and led her back to the vehicle. "If any shooting starts, lie down on the floor."

She nodded and let him help her down. The sergeant spoke a few words to the major inside, and the door opened. "Major Pettigrew, here is Miss Blue Eye," he said. "Take care of her, sir."

The major ignored Mary, and she would have been fine with that, except that such a stance seemed almost cowardly. She took a deep breath and decided to make conversation. As they traveled that notorious part of the trail, Mary decided she had been hasty in thinking ill of the paymaster, who, she learned, had a wife back East he saw now and then and two grandchildren.

She was well on her way to telling him more about her father, a Dartmouth graduate who served as Judge Wilkins's secretary, and

Mama, who cooked, when the driver set the brake and Sergeant Blade opened the door.

"I believe we'll arrive at Hunton's stage station with all our hair," he said. "Thank you, Major Pettigrew. I trust Miss Blue Eye wasn't unruly or demanding?"

"Not at all," the paymaster replied. "In fact, if she'd rather stay with me . . ."

"Your choice," Rowan said to her.

"The point is, I had a choice," she told the sergeant a few minutes later after she had thanked the major prettily and resumed her place atop a horse that didn't mind a sidesaddle or an Indian.

"That's all anyone wants," he said. "The major decided you weren't a fearsome creature?"

She knew he was teasing her, but Mary saw something else in his firm expression. Funny that she had ever thought him formidable.

"I never was," she said.

He smiled at that. Maybe it was his turn to feel shy.

# SIX

HUNTON'S STAGE STATION was as noisy as Mary remembered it from her trip to Fort Laramie. With few travelers in late October, she had a curtained-off partition to herself, which was all the luxury anyone could expect. His eyes on some barely sober cowboys, Sergeant Blade posted a guard outside her curtain, which turned out to be him and then the corporal halfway through the night. Mary slept better than she thought she would.

They left at dawn, making a steady push that saw them to Cheyenne at dusk, just as the eastbound train pulled in to the Union Pacific depot. Sergeant Blade retrieved the calico money from the military strongbox and sent the paymaster on his way rejoicing.

Earlier that afternoon, another Indian scare meant the major heard the whole story of the calico ball when Mary joined him in the ambulance again.

At his request, she told the paymaster some favorite longhouse stories and answered his questions about life on the still-shrinking Seneca reservation. In turn he assured her that her relatives had almost nothing in common with western hostiles. She could have told him that earlier, when he chose not to share his ambulance. She decided the paymaster was better informed now, and she could be charitable.

Mary also arrived at an unexpected personal judgment. The only daughter with three older brothers, she had been raised by doting parents. Perhaps, just perhaps, she had been spoiled as much as Victoria Masterson. Perhaps it was time to grow up and face the fact that while she did not live in a perfect world, she could whine less about her own lot in life.

And so Major Pettigrew had given her a courtly bow at the depot and told Sergeant

Blade to take care of "this charming little lady."

"You made a friend, charming lady," Rowan teased as they watched the train leave. He glanced at Mary. "I feared you would hop the train and head East yourself, and how could I ever explain that to my superiors?"

"I thought about it," she told him as they walked back to the troopers holding their horses. "I promised Mama I would weather out six months." She had to smile. "I find it singularly amusing that during a short jaunt to Cheyenne I became a 'charming little lady.'"

Sergeant Blade laughed at that as they rode along together. He sent the rest of the troop through to Fort Russell with the corporal. His face changed to the more serious expression she also knew. "I wish that all of us out here, white and Indian alike, had the luxury of such a discovery. Until that happens . . . Follow my lead here, if you will, and trust me not to be a scoundrel."

Mary mulled over his words as he dismounted in front of the Plainsmen Hotel and helped her down. Sergeant Blade escorted her into the lobby, calmly signed the register as Sergeant and Mrs. Rowan Blade, then handed her the single room key after the clerk finished and before her blushing confusion subsided.

"I didn't want to chance the clerk getting all huffy about Blue Eye and denying you a room," he said quietly. "It's a serviceable falsehood, and after all, unlike our major, he hasn't had the benefit of your company, has he? I'll meet you in the dining room over there at eight tomorrow morning, and we will scavenge the dry goods stores in town."

"I must pay you for the room," Mary said, and opened her purse.

"Captain Hayes already did," Rowan said. "He told me to make certain you had safe accommodations in Cheyenne. It was his contribution to this bit of female silliness, I believe was how he put it." He leaned toward her, a surprising conspirator. "Captain Hayes is, unlike his wife, not a foolish person." He put a forefinger to his forage cap. "Until tomorrow, Miss Blue Eye."

Sergeant Blade wasn't a man to argue with, so she didn't try. Maybe he was right in camouflaging her and protecting her behind his own name. The clerk appeared none the wiser, and must have thought they were married. She could think about Rowan's Gordian Knot way of solving a problem later, perhaps when she was riding home to New York on that eastbound train.

If that was still her plan. During a solitary dinner and then a peaceful evening in a pleasant room, Mary thought about Major Pettigrew. He hadn't apologized for his bigotry, but the major had changed. So had she. How much, she wasn't certain. As she drifted off to sleep, Mary Blue Eye considered that the answer to her question wouldn't be discovered if she ran back home when times were tough.

# SEVEN

MAMA HAD WARNED her that when it came to shopping, men were never the best companions. Mary made an exception for Sergeant Blade, who arrived promptly at eight o'clock in time for breakfast, which he admitted was his second one of the day, and better tasting than the first.

A waiter appeared when the sergeant sat down. After a brief negotiation, the man hurried away and returned promptly with two fried eggs, a mound of bacon, and toast.

"I could eat breakfast all day," he told Mary as he tucked in.

Mary smiled at him, thinking about this odd situation, sharing breakfast with an amiable man, who, if she gauged the admiring glances of female diners properly, was someone to look at once or twice.

Maybe it was the impeccable cut of his uniform, or possibly his excellent posture, acquired through years in the saddle. He had a satisfying tan just starting to fade with the changing of the season. Mary decided that it should be against the law for any man except a trooper to wear a moustache that drooped at the corners. She glanced around and saw no other man with shoulders so broad. She thought Rowan's face a little thin, but that seemed to be coin of the realm in the cavalry.

Knowing it was too much to hope he would go with her to pick out fabric, Mary felt generous enough to provide an exit, should he want one. "You needn't accompany me from store to store," she said cautiously. "Mama warned me about men and shopping."

That earned a hearty laugh from her dining companion. "Mary, I am made of sterner stuff than that," he assured her. "If you don't ask me to select a hat for you, or ask my opinion on something related to women's finery, we will manage."

"Very well, sir." She could laugh inside about that artless comment. Indians were good at laughing inside.

"Besides, I have commandeered the ambulance. How were *you* planning to haul enough fabric for fifteen dresses?"

She hadn't thought of that. "Did you commandeer a driver, too?"

"I did. He is in the ambulance, currently sleeping off a prodigious drunk."

"I probably should draw a curtain over this conversation, shouldn't I?"

"Perhaps. Let us say that when he wakes up and discovers he is not in the guardhouse, he will thank me." He touched her hand. "And *that* is the secret to leadership."

Cheyenne's Fifteenth Street featured more saloons than dry goods stores, but the sergeant shepherded his charge past still-shuttered bars to the quieter cross streets away from the depot. As if ready to spar with each other, the Cheyenne Mercantile Emporium and the less abundantly named Wyoming Dry Goods faced each other across a wide dirt street.

"Coin toss?" Rowan asked.

“Wyoming Dry Goods,” Mary told him. “I have a good feeling about it.”

Inside a cool interior featuring the tang of dried herring mixed with hair oil, the sergeant nodded approvingly. “I suppose ladies have an instinct about these things. I bow to your superior knowledge.”

Her choice of stores was only the merest luck, but he didn’t need to know that. They stood in front of a shelf boasting at least seven different fabric colors and designs. It was still a far cry from what she might have chosen from back home, but this was Wyoming Territory and not New York.

A dapper man in a white shirt and canvas apron, with a tape measure draped around his neck stood behind the counter. Mary felt herself leaning back as he looked her over, found her massively wanting, ignored her, and turned his attention to Sergeant Blade. Maybe she *didn’t* have an instinct about Wyoming Dry Goods after all.

She knew what the sergeant would do before he did it, which nearly brought tears to her eyes. He casually put his arm around Mary’s shoulders and drew her close to his side. "My wife and I have been sent to buy fabric for a calico ball at Fort Laramie," he said. "How many yards per dress, my dear?"

"Ten," she said calmly, as if Sergeant Blade spoke to her that way from dawn to dusk. Peace covered her right down to her soul. "The fabric is thirty-six inches wide?"

"Yes, ma'am," the clerk said promptly, after a quick look at the sergeant, who had leveled him with the same stare Mary had noticed Rowan use when leading particularly inept recruits through equitation on the parade ground.

Rowan released her and tapped his knuckles lightly on the counter, which seemed to unnerve the clerk. *You've made your point*, Mary thought, amused. "I can manage now, Rowan," she said. "We could probably use a sack or two of peppermints. I think your troopers have earned it, don't you?"

"Mary, you're a wonder," he said. "Good thing we brought you along." He tapped the counter again, once and hard. The clerk dropped the tape measure. "If you have any difficulty, my dear, just sing out." He walked toward the front of the store, looking back twice, which made the now totally unmanned clerk gulp audibly.

"He likes to make certain I have good service," she told the clerk. "Ten yards of each of these calicos, and then I'll need thread and boning."

Mary doubted any female patron in Wyoming Dry Goods had ever received such excellent service. They had similar luck across the street at the more grandiose Mercantile Emporium, once the sergeant established his connection with Mary Blue Eye in a way that no one would dream of questioning.

"I believe we are done," Mary said, after a lengthy time watching another terrified clerk measure and cut. "I imagine that will come as a relief to you."

"Not necessarily," Rowan said as he picked up the twine-tied bundle of fabric as if it weighed nothing, and counterbalanced it with the fabric he already carried from Wyoming Dry Goods. "Did you find some calico for yourself?"

"I never even considered that I would be dancing, too," Mary said when they stood on the street. She took a long look at all the fabric. "I wager I will be sewing dresses right up to the ball itself. No time."

He set down both heavy parcels. "That won't do. May I escort you to the ball?"

"*Me*?"

The sergeant looked around elaborately. "I don't know anyone else on this street."

"I never thought . . ."

He picked up the bundles, then set them down again, as if he had arrived at some momentous decision. He put his hands on her shoulders. "I watched you on that first day of the trip to Fort Laramie. I saw the excitement in your eyes. In the last few months I have watched it diminish. What happened to that little lady?"

"You've been watching me?"

"I watch everyone connected in any way with G Troop," he said. "Soldiers and dependents alike." Astounded, Mary watched the lift and fall of his shoulders. "I watch you with those silly wives. I know you are being taken advantage of, and there isn't anything I can do about it."

Why did he have to say that? Tears

welled in her eyes and spilled down her cheeks. He pulled her close right there and let her babble into his overcoat about her tiresome and childish friend and the huge gulf between them now. Keeping her voice low, she raged against the realization that the officers' wives saw her as someone biddable who would sew and do all that was expected of her because she was an Indian and a servant.

"It's not just the officers' wives," she said. "The corporal's wife who cooks for the Mastersons gets her digs in, too, that I am lazy and ignorant."

Mary thought about that a moment, until her innate honesty took over. "She might be right. I should know more about cooking."

"Are you the youngest in your family?" he asked.

She nodded. "Youngest and the only daughter. I might have been spoiled a little."

"Perhaps, but nothing prepared you for . . . this."

"No," she said, and felt her frustration dribble away. Maybe proximity to a man disinclined to judge her was soothing the wound no one could see. "They don't know anything about me," she concluded, embarrassed now. She backed away and he let her go. Maybe it was time for her own confession.

"And do you know something else? I see the Indians at Fort Laramie, the ones called Laramie Loafers. I watch the Indian mothers begging with their eyes. I see them in rags, and I feel superior to them. I am not, am I?"

Sergeant Blade picked up the fabric, his face serious. "None of us are. That's why I hate my job, at times."

She touched his arm and gestured at the calico bundles he carried. "This calico would make a lot of dresses, aprons, and children's shirts for the sad people hanging about the fort. I ask myself, why not start charity at home?"

"That, my dear, is a question for the ages," he replied. "Why not? Wait here. I'm going to put this fabric in the ambulance, check on my driver, and take you one more place."

# Eight

Mary was amazed that he wanted anything to do with her, after she had cried all over his greatcoat and made a spectacle of herself. She looked around cautiously, happy to see no one else on the street except two cowboys arguing in front of one of the saloons, and an old dog scratching himself and looking supremely indifferent.

"Where are we going?" she asked when he returned from the ambulance and offered his arm.

"There's a dressmaker I know . . ."

"You know a dressmaker?" Was this man always going to surprise her?

"Her brother was a corporal in the Tenth Cavalry, a Negro regiment," he said as they walked along. "I taught him to read, and he made sergeant. My Fifth and his Tenth were garrisoned at Fort Davis in Texas."

"He couldn't *read*?"

"Mary, he spent the first twenty years of his life as a slave on a Louisiana plantation. Reading was against the law."

"At least that never happened to Indians," she said.

"He came up to me one morning after guard mount and asked me if I would teach him. Said his lieutenant told him he could make sergeant if he could read the manual of arms, call roll, and fill out reports."

"Why did he ask you?"

Mary watched the color rise from the sergeant's neck to bloom on his face. "It can't be that embarrassing, Rowan."

"Maybe not to you . . . He said I had a kind face, and there weren't too many of those at Fort Davis," Rowan said, after taking his turn to look around. "A sergeant with a kind face . . . I didn't know what to say. Well, except yes, of course I would help him. And I did. He's a first sergeant now. His sister used to live with him before she married a railroad man."

He appeared disinclined to say more, which suited Mary well enough. It was still before noon, and she had already examined her motives and character in light of the uncomfortable reality that she was probably as spoiled, in her own way, as Victoria Masterson, and also sadly lacking. Why Sergeant Blade continued to be so kind to her was a question for the ages.

One short block and one more took them nearly out of Cheyenne. Rowan stopped in front of a modest clapboard house with a sign in the front window: *Mrs. William Washington, Dressmaker.*

"Sukey told me that she wrote *Modiste* first, but no one in Cheyenne knew what that was," Sergeant Blade told Mary. "This is more of a dressmaker kind of town." He knocked on the door, listened, then opened it and ushered her inside.

Mary looked around in delight at the neat-as-a-pin parlor on one side and the business side with its cutting table, Singer, and mannequin wearing a dress she would happily commit a felony to own, if she thought she could get away with it.

"My goodness, but I want that dress," she told Rowan, who laughed, then swept off his forage cap when a tall, supremely elegant black woman came into the room, tape measure around her neck, shears in her hand, and a smile of welcome on her face.

"Sukey Washington, are you ever going to look a day over twenty?" he asked, by way of greeting. "And where is that useless husband who should protect you from scoundrels like me?"

The dressmaker laughed. "Sergeant Blade, he's down at the railyard, and you know precisely how old I am!" she exclaimed. "My goodness, did you finally do the wise thing and marry?"

*I won't look at him, I won't look at him*, Mary told herself as her own face turned rosy enough for two people.

Sukey Washington glanced from Rowan to Mary and back. She rolled her eyes. "Forgive me, then, for assuming, but who is this lovely lady?"

That was all the impetus the sergeant needed to draw a deep breath and move right along. “This is Miss Mary Blue Eye. We have quite a story to tell, haven’t we, Mary?”

If she lived to be eighty, Mary knew she would never forget the sweetness that was Sukey Washington. After enduring months now of wary looks and second glances as people wondered just who and what she was, this dark woman gazed at her with no guile and no hesitation.

“Blue Eye. What a beautiful name,” she said.

“I have always thought so,” Mary replied, then couldn’t help herself. “At least until I came out West. It’s kind of hard here.” And then she horrified herself by bursting into tears again.

Feeling helpless and stupid, Mary turned for the door. She could wait outside while the sergeant visited with his friend. Why was she so foolish?

She got no farther than the thought.

“My goodness.” Sukey Washington put her arms around Mary. “It’s not easy, is it?”

“I don’t mean to be a baby,” Mary said when she could speak. Sukey was soft and comfortable, and she never wanted to move.

"I'm tired of people looking at me. I really don't want to sew fifteen dresses, even though I have to." She stepped away. "Here I am telling you this when you already know how it is. I'm sorry. Forgive me."

Sukey pulled her close again. "A hurt is a hurt. I also wish people could see the me that I see."

Mary nodded. *The me that I see*, she thought. *Yes, that's it.*

She blew her nose and felt herself in control, even if too immature to be seen around grown-ups. "Let me wait outside while you visit with Sergeant Blade. I'm sorry I was so childish."

"Stay here," Rowan said. "I wanted to say hello, but also to ask Sukey if she has any calico."

"We already have what we need," Mary reminded him.

"But no fabric for you. I still want you to go to the calico ball with me."

Oh dear, he hadn't forgotten. "I have too many dresses to sew, Sergeant. Thank you, though, for the invitation."

"What do you have here?" he asked Sukey, obviously intending to ignore Mary.

"Follow me."

He did and motioned for Mary to come too. She shook her head, and he gave her what was probably a kinder version of The Stare.

"Very well, although I do not have time to sew." She might have been a cricket chirping on the hearth, for all the attention he paid.

Still, a lovely bolt of cloth caught her eye, one of five equally lovely ones stacked next to more expensive fabrics. She couldn't help her sigh of appreciation.

How strange that the sergeant pointed to the same bolt. Sukey pulled it out from between two others and carried it into the front room. She stretched out two yards, then looked from Mary to the material and back.

"I wouldn't have thought this, but dark blue with white polka dots is perfect for your complexion," Sukey said. She held up the fabric to Mary's face. "And black hair? My dear, you were born to wear this."

Sergeant Blade was reaching in his back

pocket. Mary stopped him, her hand on his arm.

"You will not pay for this, Sergeant Blade," Mary said, and gave him what she hoped was an approximation of The Stare. "I will."

Their stare-down lasted a few seconds, and she won. He held his hands up.

Her eyes lively, Sukey named a price. Mary said, "Ten yards," and handed over her own money.

"I personally hope that was your train fare back East money," he whispered in Mary's ear while Sukey cut the fabric, humming to herself.

"I'm keeping my ticket money safe," Mary replied, flattered that it mattered to him.

"You know you'll miss me," he teased.

*I believe I will*, she thought.

"You'll let me carry your purchase, Miss Blue Eye?" the sergeant asked most formally, humor in his eyes, too, once they were on the street again, after tea with Sukey Washington and sandwiches to take along.

"Certainly you may," Mary replied. She took a deep breath. "And yes, I will go to the calico ball with you."

# NINE

THE AMBULANCE STAYED behind at Fort Russell and was replaced by a wagon containing mainly requisitioned supplies. Rowan wrapped the formidable mound of fabric for the calico ball in burlap and set it next to Mary's valise and bedroll, made from three of the pile of army blankets requisitioned for Fort Laramie.

Sergeant Blade tried to politely talk her out of riding sidesaddle, citing blustery weather and the hint of snow. She said it would take more than that to coop her up into a supply wagon with kegs of dried beef, red paint in tins, and surprisingly, even more dried raisins.

He finally shared news Mary didn't want

to hear. "A patrol in this morning from Fort Fetterman crossed a big trail of Indian ponies headed north. I'd rather you stayed in the wagon."

Mary knew better than to argue. He added that the troopers had noticed the straight lines denoting travois, which usually meant women and children.

"It's no raiding party, Mary."

"Maybe we can give them some of the raisins," she joked.

"The logic here, Miss Smarty, is to cut a low profile and avoid what looks like a sizeable party, even if they aren't bent on raiding," he said. "The wagon for you."

"And if we surprise them by accident?"

"You're determined to worry, aren't you?"

"I like to know where I stand."

"If we surprise them, it won't be pretty," he admitted. "Trust me to keep you safe."

Maybe a joke would help. "You'd better, because I have fifteen dresses to make."

"Sixteen. Don't forget yours," Rowan reminded her.

Mary made herself comfortable by

adding a few blankets to her stash in the wagon. Someone had put in a pile of newspapers, the *Chicago Tribune* among them, probably intended for enlisted men's day rooms and officers with subscriptions. She fished out the Tribs and settled in for a day reading about the Great Chicago Fire, as it was already being called, along with "One for the history books," and "A conflagration such as we have never seen, and we have seen a lot."

She spent the afternoon reading through pages of first-person accounts of the "raging inferno unequalled in all the annals of the United States," shaking her head over loss of life and stories of families searching for children unaccounted for and hotheads ready to lynch all Irishmen because of Mrs. O'Leary's cow. Sukey Washington's sandwiches went down with ease, and so did the handful of raisins Mary knew no sharp-eyed commissary clerk would miss.

She had just started an article detailing what the various churches were doing to relieve the suffering poor when she heard

Sergeant Blade holler, “Close up, men, we’re in for it.”

The teamster turned to her. “Head down,” he ordered. “Hang on.”

From the time she was small, her parents had taught her instant obedience. Her college-educated father had apologized for the lesson. “Nothing more will ever happen here to our Seneca Nation because it has all been done to us,” he had told her. “Even then, my father so taught me, and his father before him, going back and back. When someone tells you to obey, you obey.”

“Nëga:je:” Mary heard Papa speak to her from that corner of her mind called Seneca wisdom, the one she hadn’t visited much. She sank to the wagon bed. “I will try,” she repeated in English as she wedged herself between two kegs.

After trundling down and up through what she thought must be the Chugwater to the opposite bank, they headed on a run toward a higher point, then stopped with a lurch. She heard the teamster set the brake, then leap into the wagon bed with her. He rested his Sharps carbine against the wagon seat he had just vacated.

"Doing okay, missy?" he asked, his eyes forward on what, mercifully, she could not see.

"Doing okay," she echoed.

She heard horses close to the wagon and the creak of leather as men dismounted. "What is happening?" she asked the driver, hoping she didn't sound as frightened as she felt.

"There aren't enough of us to allow one in four to hold the horses while the rest of the troopers dismount and fight," he explained, then stopped to squeeze off a shot. "They've tied the horses to the wagon wheels. Glad I set the brake."

Another shot. A gasp. The murmur of voices. Sobbing and then silence. Her nerves tuned like fine wire, Mary heard someone fiddle with the canvas at the back of the wagon and flinched as the tailgate dropped.

"Help me, Casey."

She knew the sergeant's voice, marveling that he sounded so calm. "Can I help, too?" she asked.

"You can. We're handing in a wounded man. Casey will pull him toward you. Do what you can to stop the bleeding."

She waited for the teamster to crawl toward the bleeding trooper that Rowan pushed inside as gently as he could, considering.

"Degadënö:nyöh," she said.

"Come again?" Rowan asked.

"Just thanking my parents for teaching me things they thought I would never need," she told him.

"And I thank them, too," the sergeant said. "Keep your head down. We'll get through this." He slammed up the tailgate and jerked down the canvas.

The trooper stared at her with frightened eyes. Mary could not remember his name, or if she even knew it. "Your name?"

"Will Lemaster," he said. "Can you help me?"

"I will do my best."

Casey had returned to his crouch by the wagon seat. Will tugged himself closer to her, using his elbows because his left leg seemed useless. Mary saw the blood pooling under the fleshy part of his thigh, if troopers even had fleshy parts.

"Damn but I wish it had been an arrow. They don't bleed so much at first," he said. "Can you cut off my trousers above the shot hole?"

His question jolted her into motion. Mary opened her valise and took out her cutting shears. Thank goodness she had brought them along to Cheyenne. Like a typical Easterner, she hadn't trusted a town as raw and ungainly as Cheyenne to have any such thing.

She did her best not to cause him any pain, and Will did his best not to do more than suck in his breath when she did. Her fingers were soon slippery with the trooper's blood as she cut off the trouser leg and pulled it away.

"I don't think the ball went all the way through," she said.

The trooper grimaced. "A surgeon's going to need to probe around. Right now, stop the bleeding. I can only lose so much."

She looked with some longing at the pile

of fabric that others had paid for, then returned to her valise, where she took out the beautiful dark-blue material with polka dots she had paid for a few hours ago.

She reminded herself she was leaving in January, and seriously, where would she have found the time to make that dress at all? Mary cut into the length of the material, moved the shears steadily up two yards, then cut across. Moving deliberately, her hands steady now, she folded the strip over and over until she had a respectable pad.

Another few snips and she cut more of the lovely fabric. She placed the pad over the wound weeping blood. "Hold it there," she ordered.

He did as she said, fear gone from his face. Heavens, the man must have thought she knew what she was doing.

"Hold it tight as I start the wrap," she said.

He did. After wiping her hands on her skirt, Mary wrapped the strip around the pad and his thigh until it was bound up neatly, with maximum pressure on the pad. If this didn't work, she couldn't think of anything else except a tourniquet, which even she knew would mean eventual amputation.

"Let's hope it works, Will," she said. "I've pretty well exhausted my skills."

Mary picked up the canteen Sergeant Blade must have left for her or Will and dipped another hunk of her material in it. She swabbed at the wagon bed until it was less bloody and set the brown paper down that had wrapped the fabric.

"If you can scoot onto this, it will tell us if the bandage is working," she said. "I'll help you."

She made him as comfortable as she could, with his head propped against a bag of cornmeal, then covered him with an army blanket. "It's the best I can do right now," she said. "I wish it were more."

The private leaned back with a sigh. "All things considered, Miss Blue Eye, I'm fine."

She smiled at that. "You're a liar, Will, but thank you."

"No, it's the truth," he insisted. "Just hold my hand now and then, and I'll be the envy of the entire Fifth Cavalry."

He honestly looked as though he meant

it. Mary felt herself relaxing. There wouldn't have been time to make a dress for herself anyway, and this was more important. She poured a tin cup of water from the canteen and held it to his lips, because bravado aside, his hands shook. Hers were remarkably steady. Mama would be impressed. When he finished, he sighed again and closed his eyes. "Wake me up if you need any help," he joked.

She laughed, which made Casey, still kneeling by the wagon seat, look at her in surprise. He shook his head and turned his gaze outward again.

She sat beside the sleeping private and held his hand as the firing diminished and finally stopped. Obedient to the order from Sergeant Blade and from her own caution, she waited.

"Mary? Is he still alive? How're you?"

"We're fine."

Funny thing was, they were. A most pleasant feeling had shouldered aside her apprehension. For the first time in her admittedly cosseted and comfortable life, she felt useful and needed, with the sleeping trooper not remotely concerned that she was at least some part Indian and young. It was a pleasant sensation, and she wanted more of it.

Her euphoria disappeared when Sergeant Blade threw back the canvas and dropped the tailgate again. He carried a young Sioux with his upper arm crooked at a strange angle.

"Ready to tackle another project?" Rowan asked, as casually as if he were commenting on the weather. "He fell off his horse. He's not too happy."

# TEN

"He says his name is Smooth Stone, or something like that," Rowan told her as he stood there. "Obviously he's having some trouble with sign language at the moment, what with one arm bent out of shape."

He peered into the wagon. "How's Private Lemaster doing?"

"Well enough, I think. I made a strong pad for the wound and bound it tight, but he needs a surgeon."

"We'll get him one. Help me with Mr. Smooth Stone, who I don't think is a day over twelve, if that." He sighed. "Bring along more of your fabric. We have some scrapes and nicks to bandage."

Will opened his eyes when she released

his hand. She took a moment to lift the blanket and check the brown paper. No stains, which relieved her heart and mind. "I have to help someone else," she told him. "Go back to sleep."

"I'll watch Will." The teamster leaned his carbine against the wagon seat. "Don't think he'll want to hold my hand, though."

The rest of her own material in hand and holding the shears, Mary let the corporal help her from the wagon. She leaned into the wagon for another blanket and spread it on the ground for the sergeant to deposit his burden, who looked none too pleased.

To call him twelve years old was generous. Mary would have thought closer to ten. "You're a little young to be doing this," she told him.

"Wasichu. Wasichu," Smooth Stone said.

Mary looked at Rowan and shrugged.

"I think he wants to know if you are white," Sergeant Blade said. He looked over his shoulder. "Private McIntyre, front and center."

Private McIntyre came forward, his hand against his head, blood on his fingers.

"Thought I was just going to feel the whistle as the bullet passed, but it took a little detour, Sarge." He sounded apologetic that he hadn't leaped out of the way.

"How's your Sioux, Private?"

"Not bad, Sarge," McIntyre said cheerfully. "It'll get better once the little lady lets me have a strip of that material. Pretty stuff."

"Yes, isn't it?" Sergeant Blade said drily. "Sorry, Mary."

"At this point, I don't care," she said and ripped off a strip. "Sit down. I can do this better than you."

With a glance at Rowan, who nodded, Private McIntyre sat down. Practiced now in the art of medical improvisation, Mary dabbed the bullet furrow with water, then bandaged the private's head, with the knot over the wound for best pressure. "That should do until something better comes along," she said. She looked back at Smooth Stone, who waited more or less patiently because he didn't have much choice.

"Can you tell him that I am an Indian?"

"I'll show you how to sign it," McIntyre

said. Despite what she suspected was a massive headache, he seemed to be enjoying himself.

He showed her, rubbing the back of his left hand twice with his right hand. Smooth Stone added some commentary of his own.

"He wants to know what nation."

Her nation. *I have a nation, same as Smooth Stone*, she thought. *The Keepers have traveled the path of the white man longer than the Sioux. Whether that is good or bad, who can tell?*

"My nation," she said softly. "Private, tell him I am a Keeper of the Western Door." Pride filled her heart. "Tell him I live very far away from here, to the place where the sun rises."

"Your wish is my command," McIntyre said and signed her message. "Don't know what he understands, because I'm not so good."

"Better than I," she said. Once back home, she would improve her education. The Seneca let their women speak and make decisions. She could ask to learn more and not be ignored.

When Private McIntyre finished, Smooth Stone reached out his good hand and touched Mary's hand. He said something, and she looked at McIntyre.

"'Cure,' as near as I can translate it."

"Tell him I'll do my best."

"You tell him. It's like this."

She watched the trooper, then signed. The boy closed his eyes.

"Better tell him it might hurt," she added.

"He knows that."

"I'll help you, Mary," Rowan said. "Private, get Casey to find sticks about eighteen inches long. I signed a bill of lading for window shades, so he should find some slats inside those."

Rowan ran his hand along the odd-shaped upper arm as the boy steeled himself. Gently he manipulated the area where the bone digressed from its usual path. Mary pressed her hand against Smooth Stone's chest.

"It's bent for certain, but it's not snapped off completely," Rowan said. "I think I can realign it."

Mary touched the boy's face and looked

deep into eyes much like her own. His stoicism vanished, but she saw no fear. "I want to be this brave someday."

"You already are," Rowan said. "Maybe you needed a reminder. Here goes."

It was over quickly. Smooth Stone tensed and gasped, and Mary tightened her grip. He lapsed into unconsciousness long enough for Sergeant Blade to probe a bit, then nod. Rowan cut Casey's window slats and held the boy's arm as Mary ripped off more strips of her beautiful calico and bound the arm and the improvised splint from shoulder to elbow.

Smooth Stone opened his eyes and looked at his arm. He raised it tentatively and nodded. Sergeant Blade signed, and he nodded again. Mary took another length of fabric and made a sling. Smooth Stone sat up so she could circle it around his neck and secure his forearm inside.

"We need to get him back to his people, and then I am riding for the surgeon," Rowan said. "We're much closer to Fort Russell than Laramie, and I want the surgeon to see to Private Lemaster."

"That sounds too dangerous," Mary said.

"I would have agreed, if Smooth Stone hadn't fallen off his horse and landed, so to speak, in your lap." He touched her shoulder. "Do you feel brave?" He leaned closer. "There's really only one answer, oh Keeper of the Western Door."

"Since you put it that way, yes, I feel brave," she told him, even though she didn't, not at all.

"We'll ride him back to his people. I doubt they've gone far."

"That sounds terrifying."

"Less than you think. I have no idea who Smooth Stone's parents are, but they'll be happy to see him."

"Certainly they will," Mary said. "Perhaps Private McIntyre could come along, too, if we need to say something. Would he mind?"

"You forget who he works for," Rowan said with a smile. "It'll be an order."

"Why doesn't this frighten you?" she asked.

"They weren't a war party. We surprised them, which I was afraid might happen. I believe they're Brulé, heading north to

Spotted Tail's Whetstone Agency, because winter is coming."

Rowan clapped his arm around Mary's shoulder, then turned her toward the supply wagon. "Check on Private Lemaster, if you please, and pull on your riding boots." He gestured to Private McIntyre. "Tell Smooth Stone we are returning him to his people."

# ELEVEN

MARY PULLED ON her riding boots, her eyes on Private Lemaster, who smiled faintly and returned to the half doze of a wounded man.

She stopped Casey before he swung her down from the wagon. "We should probably bring along gifts. If you don't think the army will be too upset with me, could you fill the pail with raisins? And please hand me the rest of my material and those shears."

She set the full pail beside the wagon and eyed the beautiful calico. She kept back three yards so she could change Private Lemaster's bandage, then folded the rest. Maybe Smooth Stone's mother could use it.

She let the sergeant throw her into the

saddle again, then waited while he tied the fabric to the saddle.

He swung into the saddle and held out his arms for Smooth Stone, handed up by Private McIntyre, who mounted his own horse. The sergeant wrapped Smooth Stone in an army blanket, careful not to jostle him.

"How do you know where to go?" Mary asked.

"I don't. I'm following the direction where they last fired on us," he said. "I can't help but think they haven't gone far."

They rode west through terrain that the teamster had earlier told her was perfect for buffalo and Indians. "You might think it's all level ground, but see how it dips," he had pointed out. "The whole Sioux Nation could probably hide here and we'd be none the wiser."

Down in one dip, up another, rinse and repeat, and then there they were, a gathering of Indians that made Mary suck in her breath and hope Sergeant Blade hadn't heard.

As they rode up out of the gully, a line of horsemen turned and faced them, effectively barring passage. Behind them she could make out horses pulling travois, and women with babies on their backs. She remembered that Mama still kept the beaded cradleboard into which she had popped a much younger Mary.

"It will be yours someday," Mama had said. At the time, Mary had politely refrained from shaking her head over old-fashioned ways in modern times. As she watched Lakota babies in their cradleboards, she knew she wanted that pretty thing now. It was practical and lovely, and a woman could carry her baby and have hands free for housework.

Smooth Stone was leaning forward now, straining toward his people. "We'll get you there, buddy," Sergeant Blade said.

Rowan kneed his horse ahead, and Mary and the private fell in behind. She held her breath as the warriors moved into a *v* shape and effectively funneled them toward the main body of the travelers. She heard the horses and riders closing the gap once they passed through.

One warrior came close enough to strike Sergeant Blade on his shoulder, then cup that same hand against Smooth Stone's cheek. He smiled, and Mary let out the breath she had been holding.

"Imagine that. He just counted coup on me," Rowan told her. "Here goes."

He pulled back the army blanket so Smooth Stone's father could see his son's splinted arm and sling. "He fell pretty hard," Rowan said.

Private McIntyre started to translate, but the warrior held up his hand. "I understand," he said slowly, as if he were trying out his English for the first time in a while. "He is too young, but he argues. His mother wanted to kill me."

Sergeant Blade laughed at that, and the warrior smiled. Between the father and the sergeant, they lowered the boy carefully to the ground.

Rowan dismounted next, then held his arms out for Mary, who lifted her leg over the upper pommel and let him help her down. She touched Smooth Stone's shoulder. "He was very brave and did not cry out once," she said.

The warrior made no comment to her but turned at another sound. A woman had dismounted and pushed her way through the warriors. Mary tried not to smile as she shook her finger at Smooth Stone, said something succinct that needed no translation, then carefully pulled him close.

Mary glanced at Rowan, who watched the whole scenario with appreciation all over his face, mingled with relief.

"We should probably go now," the sergeant said. "You know, while the going's good."

Mary nodded. It was enough to see Smooth Stone back where he belonged and to get her first up close glimpse of the power and might of the Sioux. She wondered if her own people had once looked this way. Now the Seneca were farmers and clerks like her own father, living different lives. Again she felt a strong urge to know more about her own.

"I have gifts," she said to Rowan. She unhooked the pail from the saddle and untied the fabric from its binding. Gifts in hand, she held out the raisins to Smooth Stone's mother.

Mary handed her the fabric next, which made her eyes widen in appreciation. The woman smoothed down the fabric, then put it to her cheek. She held it up against Mary's face and took a good look. She spoke to her husband, who cleared his throat against more English.

"Woman asks, who are your people?"

"I am a daughter of the Keepers of the Western Door," she said, pointing east. "We are of the Iroquois League, many, many sleeps that way. I am Mary Blue Eye."

He nodded and told his wife, who came closer, pressed her forehead against Mary's, and looked into her eyes. She spoke to her husband, who laughed and said, "No blue."

"It is an old family name," Mary said. "I am proud of my people."

"Good for you, Mary," Rowan said. He looked around. "Let us see if we can extricate ourselves gracefully. Personally, I think Smooth Stone should stand in a corner for a while, if tipis had corners."

"Oh, you!"

"We need to leave, and you need to be on your way," Rowan told the warrior.

The father held up his hand to stop them because his wife was whispering to him with some energy. He answered and she hurried away.

"Now we wait," he said.

Did nothing faze Sergeant Blade? Looking as casual as if the warrior sat in a parlor chatting about the weather, he asked, "Are you going toward Spotted Tail's camp?"

"We are. The winter moon comes soon." The warrior gestured overhead and made the obvious sign for birds. "In the moon of green leaves, we will return to seek buffalo."

"May you have good hunting," Sergeant Blade said. "Look, Mary."

Smooth Stone's mother had returned quietly. Shy, head down, she held out a small deerskin pouch on a leather cord. She gestured for Mary to bend down.

Mary did as she asked, and the woman put the pouch around her neck. Mary admired the quillwork on the small bag. "How do I sign 'thank you'?" she whispered to Rowan.

He showed her, and she made the sign. "What is it for?" she asked Smooth Stone's father.

"Good medicine," he said. "Thank you for my son." His voice hardened. "The Crow or Arikara would not have brought him back."

The warrior turned away and mounted his horse. His wife walked alongside him, her hand firmly on Smooth Stone's neck. The other warriors followed, and soon the three of them were alone again.

"They just vanish," Mary said.

Sergeant Blade helped her into the saddle. She breathed deep of the deerskin and touched the buttery softness of the pouch.

"What's my good medicine?" she asked Rowan.

"Whatever makes you happy," he replied and mounted.

They rode back to their makeshift bivouac in silence. Private McIntyre peeled off to join the other troopers standing by a fire. Mary smelled coffee.

"I'm taking two troopers with me to Fort Russell," he told her, after helping her down. "There might be cloth blown into Private Lemaster's wound. The surgeon will take him back to Russell and probe around a bit. He doesn't need an infection."

"But … but … you don't know that those Indians will not hang around here and try again," she said. He couldn't be seriously thinking of leaving them.

"They are not going to bother us," he said. "Don't worry, Mary. My corporal is in charge, and I have taught him everything I know."

"It's not me. What about *you*? Can't you send someone else for the surgeon?"

He seemed genuinely surprised at her concern. "What kind of a leader would that make me? Hey, don't worry."

He prepared to mount again, then stopped and looked down at his uniform. She had noticed earlier that one of his brass buttons was starting to dangle on its thread. As she watched, he worked the button loose, leaned close to open the pouch around her neck, and dropped it in.

"It's only twenty miles. Think of me, Keeper of the Western Door, and I'll be safe."

# Twelve

Private Lemaster appeared to be sound asleep in the wagon, so Mary indulged in a bout of quiet tears as the three soldiers rode away. She touched the pouch, then rubbed it against her cheek and stowed it out of sight inside her shirtwaist.

"Miss Blue Eye, we have some hardtack and sow belly. Do you want to eat it in the wagon?"

"I'll be right out," she whispered to the corporal, so as not to wake the sleeping private. Lemaster startled her by opening his eyes.

He grinned at her and said, "Shhh."

She ate quickly by the fire, happy to warm her hands around a tin cup of mashed hardtack and bacon, with a sprinkle of salt. It tasted better than she thought it would.

She took a similar tin cup to Private Lemaster, who grimaced and rose up on one elbow to eat. He shook his head over more than three spoonfuls, wanting water instead. He drank with his eyes closed and her arm under his neck. "That'll do," he said finally. She laid his head back on the cornmeal sack, and he sighed. She didn't want to alarm him, so she said nothing about the flush on his cheeks and his warmth.

She moved slightly, mostly to make herself more comfortable, but he must have thought she was leaving. He put his hand out to stop her, and she held it. He *was* warm.

"I'm staying here," she said. "I wish I could make you some chicken soup. My mother calls it the white man's elixir."

He smiled at that, but just barely. "I've thought about reenlisting, because my five is almost up, but by golly, I miss Maine."

"Five years for one enlistment?"

"Yep."

"Sergeant Blade has two stripes on his

sleeve. Does that mean ten years?" she asked, curious.

"Yep. He started pretty young in the war and stayed in. I think he's about due to reenlist." He closed his eyes. "Said he's been thinking about getting out."

"What would he do?"

He opened his eyes at her question. "My word, oh, wait, you haven't been here in the spring, have you?"

*And I won't be, either*, she thought. "What does he do in the spring?"

"Anytime there is an extra-duty detail that involves building or making cabinets, Sarge gets put in charge of the extra-duty men. Doesn't matter where we are—Fort Davis, Fort Abercrombie, Fort Shaw . . ." His voice trailed off, then came back. "He can build anything." His eyes closed and he slept this time.

Her worry grew as his fever mounted. The corporal brought her more water, and she continued to wipe Will Lemaster's face and neck. She wanted to check under his bandage but contented herself with touching the lovely calico she had wound around his thigh. It was dry, and there was no fresh blood on the brown paper underneath. She would have done more if she had known what to do, even as she admitted to herself she had nothing to do anything with. Rowan had been right to ride for the surgeon.

The one bright spot in the long afternoon came at dusk. She heard horses approaching and sat up, thinking that somehow the surgeon at Fort Russell had got the message through mental telepathy and rushed on ahead. That was stupid, but she indulged herself because she was Mary Blue Eye and never minded laughing at herself.

"Mary . . . Miss Blue Eye . . . come out now," she heard the corporal call.

She climbed out of the wagon and stared up at Smooth Stone's mother and father. "Hello," she said, not afraid.

"Hello you," the warrior said. "Shell gives this." His wife handed down a parfleche even more beautiful than the one Lieutenant Masterson wanted to hang on the wall in their quarters, though Victoria wouldn't allow it. "Take."

She took, and it was heavy. She opened it

and saw a large hunk of meat wrapped in what looked like deerskin, so it would not drip on the parfleche.

"Good food," the warrior signed, hand straight out from his heart, then fingers to his lips.

He handed down the empty pail. "Wait," Mary said and climbed back in the wagon. She scooped out more raisins, all the while thinking how good that meat would taste and what nice broth there would be for Private Lemaster. She held up the full pail to Shell, who took it with a smile.

Mary stepped back, her heart full, wishing she could say something to them, or sign something. To her further surprise, Shell leaned down and handed her one elk tooth. She pantomimed for Mary to put it in her medicine pouch.

Mary pulled the pouch from her shirtwaist and dropped in the elk tooth. On a whim, she took out Sergeant Blade's brass button and showed Shell, who put her hand to her mouth, her eyes lively. She spoke to her husband.

"Good man blue coat," he said. "Put your blanket around him."

She nodded, fully aware what he meant because she remembered a longhouse story told when Mama thought she slept. Mary stood beside the wagon until her benefactors were out of sight, then handed the meat to the corporal, who whistled and exclaimed, "No sow belly tonight, men!" He bowed elaborately. "With your permission, Miss Blue Eye."

"You have it," she said, her heart so full that the good feeling seeped into her soul, too, where she needed it even more. "Save some broth for Private Lemaster, if you please."

Will ate a little, then shook his head. One of the connoisseurs in G Troop told Mary it was elk meat, as good as any *he* ever ate. "You have some friends there, Miss Blue Eye," the private told her. She saw respect in his eyes and friendship, all she ever wanted.

After Casey saw to Private Lemaster's basic needs, Mary climbed back into the wagon and stayed the night by his side, holding his hand, praying, dozing when she could, and wiping his face. He never complained. When daybreak came and she heard what sounded like a wagon and a troop of horses, she closed her eyes in weariness and gratitude.

Mere minutes later, Captain Julius Patzki from Fort Russell introduced himself first like the Polish gentleman he was, then climbed into the wagon. He nodded to her, his eyes on his patient, lying as comfortable as Mary could make him. With her help, the surgeon peeled back the calico bandage.

"Lovely fabric, Miss Blue Eye," he said. "Sergeant Blade told me he picked it out. What talent in a sergeant."

Mary laughed. Why feel shy or reticent around a surgeon as they crouched beside a grown man's bare leg? "It was intended for a calico ball," she said. "The ladies at Fort Laramie want to help the women rendered homeless by the Chicago Fire."

Maybe it was the way she said it. Papa had chided her once about her sly humor. Captain Patzki sat back on his heels and gave her his attention. "I sense some skepticism."

"Captain, people need help right here."

"They do. I wish you all success in trying to convince some officers' wives of that," he said. He looked down at Private Lemaster. "I'm taking you back to Russell. I think there is some cloth festering in the wound, and I need to get it out." He patted the private's shoulder. "You'll feel better when I'm done."

"I'd feel braver if you came along," Lemaster told Mary.

"I wish I could, but if I don't get back to Fort Laramie and start sewing, things will get ugly with the wives of your commanding officers," she joked.

"Take good care of Sarge."

Her traitor face felt warm. "I think he can take care of himself."

"Not really." Private Lemaster closed his eyes.

Come to think of it, where was the sergeant? Mary got out of the wagon so two troopers carrying the stretcher could climb in. She looked around. No sergeant.

"Please, sir, where is Sergeant Blade?" she asked the surgeon, hoping to sound offhand and casual.

"He said he had some paperwork at the fort and then something to do in town." The surgeon turned to the corporal. "He told me you are to start out and he will catch up."

"But . . . but we were set upon by Indians only yesterday," Mary said. "Surely it isn't safe to just . . . just . . . go off and leave him."

"He told me about the Sioux. Miss Blue Eye, you are quite the asset. He also told me you would worry."

Tears filled her eyes, which probably would have startled any man except a surgeon. He touched her shoulder. "He didn't mention you would worry *that* much. He has two privates with him."

Captain Patzki turned his attention to his patient. "I promise to take good care of Private Lemaster," he told her over his shoulder, and she had to be content with that.

But she wasn't. All her mental lectures about being a little braver did her no good, and it must have showed on her face. In the middle of the afternoon, the corporal rode back by the supply wagon and took a look at her.

"He'll be around by the time we get to Hunton's," he promised.

"He had better," Mary replied. "He has

no idea that the Iroquois League, of which I am a member, raised scalping to an art form."

The teamster she sat beside laughed so loud that the troopers riding ahead turned around and joined in the laughter, even if they hadn't heard her joke. It *was* funny. Mary laughed along with him and considered it another lesson learned. She would grow up one way or another.

Looking both tired and dirty, Sergeant Blade and the two privates showed up at Hunton's as the proprietor was passing a platter of fried chicken down the table.

"I was about ready to start gnawing on my left leg," the sergeant said to the corporal, who grinned at him and made space on the bench. "How are you, gents?"

His men chuckled and continued with the weighty business of chicken, canned green beans, and biscuits in front of them. "And you, Miss Mary Blue Eye?" he added. "I passed Captain Patzki, and he had nothing but compliments for your nursing and the calico bandage."

She wanted to smile and toss off a joke

like the others, but there was no stopping the tears of relief that slid down her face. She bowed her head and let them fall quietly, another lesson learned from Mama. No Seneca ever made any noisy tears. Her tears dropped on the oilcloth in a suddenly silent room.

"I'm sorry. I was worried," she said simply, as she stared at the plate in front of her.

"Oh, Mary," was all the sergeant said.

# Thirteen

THE ROOM WAS too small. Mary excused herself and made a beeline for the back door. *You never have to leave New York again, once you get home*, she reminded herself. *Someone else can keep that western door.*

What a relief it was to step outside and take a deep breath of . . . corral. Mary shook her head at her own folly and walked around to the bench by the front entrance. She toed the spittoon out of sight under the bench and sat down, trying to pretend she was on her own front porch, snapping green beans with Mama.

Sergeant Blade was so quiet. She started when he sat down beside her, then turned her head away, embarrassed. "I really was worried for you," she said finally.

"I was, too," he admitted, "right up until Mrs. Shell gave you that medicine pouch."

She had to smile at that. Who wouldn't?

"Let me fill you in on Shell," Rowan said. "After I routed out Captain Patzki, I went to the barracks where I knew another troop of the Fifth was quartered. When I told Thad Mueller—he's another sergeant—about the whole experience and mentioned Smooth Stone and Shell, his eyes nearly bugged out."

"Why?"

"She's the favorite wife of His Pony, quite the warrior among the Brulé." He moved closer to her on the bench. "Rest assured that no one in that jolly band would have dreamed of bothering us further, not with Mr. and Mrs. His Pony on our side."

Mary produced a smile from somewhere, wondering if she could lean against his shoulder a little. She was tired of feeling alone and useful for nothing except for a minor talent in dressmaking.

She took a grand chance and leaned, which had the remarkable reflex of causing his arm to go around her shoulder as he pulled her closer. She took another chance and tipped her head against a suddenly available chest. It was just a small lean. He didn't have to think anything of it.

"I don't belong here," she said. "I'm tired of officers' wives convinced I am just another Indian in a dress and shoes, who maybe thinks she is higher in station than is legally allowed."

He chuckled at that. "Mary, they've never met anyone like you. I'll give them that, but just barely." He hesitated, as if he had his own doubts. "But you don't mind being here on this porch?"

She took another chance. "Not a bit."

He must have taken one, too, because Rowan Blade kissed her. She took another chance and kissed him back, wondering how it was that a body could feel so miserable a mere twenty seconds earlier and then feel *this* way.

The kiss came to a natural conclusion. He kept his face close to hers, which meant he was out of focus, blurry but reassuring. She knew down to her marrow that this was not a man to kiss and tease.

He sat back. "I haven't kissed a lady in ten years," he said. "My goodness, Mary Blue Eye. It's nice to feel human again."

"I've never kissed anyone before."

"Then you have a natural talent." He leaned against the bench but kept his arm around her. "I've complicated things, haven't I?"

She thought about his comment, thinking of the many times she had blurted out words that fell with a thud, and her father's patient reminder to think once, think twice, and then speak or don't. She was leaving Fort Laramie when her six months were up; she had fifteen dresses to make in two weeks; army life was never going to be to her taste. On the other hand, there was this man seated beside her.

"That remains to be seen, Rowan."

"Fair enough."

They pushed hard and arrived at Fort Laramie the next evening, just as a snowstorm of daunting proportions rolled in. Sergeant

Blade helped her from her horse and walked her to the Mastersons' quarters, two troopers carrying the fabric and her valise.

Victoria Masterson opened the door, her face wreathed in smiles to see the fabric. She told the privates to set the fabric in the dining room. When they looked around, she frowned and jabbed her forefinger at that portion of the meager sitting room designated as the dining room.

*Aren't we pretentious*, Mary thought, and felt like a servant once more.

Sergeant Blade must have noticed how her face fell. He moved closer and even stepped slightly in front of her, as if to shield her. The gesture was instinctive; she knew it.

"We had quite a return trip, Mrs. Masterson," he said. "Indians attacked, Mary tended a wounded man, and she gave away enough commissary raisins to placate a whole bunch of Brulé Sioux."

Victoria rolled her eyes. "As long as the fabric came through! No wonder Captain Hayes's wife said I should not go! Mary, we'll set up the sewing machine in the kitchen lean-to. I'm having a card party here tonight, and you would be in the way."

Humiliated, Mary walked Sergeant Blade to the porch as quickly as she could, because she saw the slow burn rising north from his uniform collar. "At least I don't have to sew outside," she joked. "Two weeks and I'll be done with those blasted dresses for a calico ball no one needs."

"I'd like to wring her neck," he said.

"That would land you in the guardhouse and then off to Fort . . . Fort somewhere."

"Leavenworth. I'm throwing you to the wolves, and I don't like it."

He stood on the porch, which meant she had to stand there, too, feeling more cheerful than he did, because she had realized something: Victoria Masterson had never been her friend. There was no point in thinking otherwise, so she needn't waste any more energy on the matter. Over and done.

"Rowan, let me tell you a longhouse story that my great-grandfather told me once when I was impatient about something I can't even remember now."

"A longhouse? You told me you live in a regular house."

"I do, but every year we travel to the longhouse, eat too much, laugh a lot, and listen to our elders tell stories. I have one for you: There was Spider, who spun a beautiful web. She would get it nearly completed, and bad-tempered Badger would break it and stomp away laughing. She began again, and the same thing happened. Over and over, she worked on her web, each part more lovely than the time before." She folded her hands in front of her. "That is the end of the story."

"That's no ending," the sergeant argued.

"It is if you are an Indian. She persisted, and so must I."

He squeezed her hand. "I'll think about that story."

Mary watched him cross the parade ground, head down against the snow, with that purposeful stride she had become accustomed to. He stood still a moment on the other side by the guardhouse, then turned and walked toward the stables. Still she watched, and smiled when he waved to her and made ushering motions, as if doing more than suggest she go inside. He was a sergeant, after all, and used to obedience.

She watched until Rowan was out of sight in the swirling snow. She thought of Shell, Smooth Stone, and His Pony and hoped they were at least close to Spotted Tail's agency.

As tired as she was, she knew she would lie in bed and think about Sergeant Blade, and getting kissed, and helping Smooth Stone, and worrying and maybe, perhaps, falling in love. Sleep could wait.

# FOURTEEN

THE FIRST THING she did in the morning was select the light-blue and yellow calico—the one for Victoria—and put the others out of sight.

Hers was a simple plan: she would make one dress at a time and not muddy up her sewing area with other calicos. When each dress was done, she would reward herself by choosing her next favorite color. She was Spider, spinning her web over and over, despite silly interruptions from Badger, also known as Victoria.

She yearned to see Sergeant Blade again, just see him. She contented herself with sewing in the lean-to and remembering his features. She had seen handsomer men, to be sure, many among her own people. What she had not noticed in those otherwise excellent men was anyone with so much capability. True, his nose was probably too long, and his lips almost but not quite chiseled enough to make any other girl take notice. His cheekbones weren't as high as hers, but not everyone could look as fine as an Indian; she was willing to make allowances.

His eyes were distinctly blue, which amused Mary no end, considering that she was the one with the Blue Eye name. He had long legs and a pleasant walk, better seen from the rear, although she would never admit that to a soul.

Mostly he was kind, not a trait his men probably saw too often, considering that he had to be a firm leader. He was kind to her, and that was what mattered.

And so Mary passed a pleasant time. When the dress-to-be turned onerous—knife pleats, boning in the basque—she let her lively mind venture deeper, to whether Sergeant Blade liked children, and whether he had much experience with women. She worked in silence and no one knew her thoughts.

Between her other duties, the first dress took her two days. At this rate, Mary knew she would still be basting pieces together while the ladies danced in petticoats and shimmies. This would never do.

How was it that Sergeant Blade seemed to know precisely when her web had been trampled by too many badgers?

She had laid out the next fabric on the parlor floor over Victoria's strenuous objections that it wasn't proper and should be done somewhere else.

"Suppose one of the other wives comes to call?" Victoria wanted to know.

Mary asked herself what Shell would do, when faced with a ninny of startling proportions, and acted. She set down her shears. "Victoria Masterson, you want these dresses. If you will not let me do it my way, I will go into my room and close the door. I never agreed to any of this. There is a Thirteenth Amendment now, and I am not your slave."

She wasn't certain which of the recent amendments had abolished slavery, but she was equally positive Victoria Masterson had no idea. She narrowed her eyes and tried to look ferocious like His Pony.

"If you must," Victoria said, after a long pause.

"I must. I have to spread out the material to cut it."

"This will go in a letter to my mother, after this wretched business is finished and I have done my duty," Victoria said with something of a flourish, as in, *So there.*

"I will take that letter to your mother when I leave here in January," Mary said, equally firm.

Oh, the panic! Oh, the sudden consternation! Victoria Masterson turned pale. "You're . . . you're . . . *leaving*?" She suddenly sounded like a child who has thrown away her favorite old doll and realizes she misses it.

"I only promised you six months."

Victoria's lips quivered. "Very well," she said, and reached for her coat. "Do what you want."

Mary sighed. Now the dratted woman was off to terrorize the captain's wife, who would carry the news of Mary's impertinence to her husband, who would do who-knew-what to placate tearful females. If that was the price of getting to use the floor to do her work, so be it.

When there came a knock on the door a half hour later, Mary looked up from her position on her hands and knees on the floor, cutting fabric. "Come in," she said, ready for the worst.

The door opened, and there stood Sergeant Blade. She sat up, her face red.

"Miss Blue Eye, you have fair terrified *your* employer. She's sobbing all over *my* employer's desk."

"Good! Maybe she will leave me alone so I can cut out material on the floor."

He shook his head. "I'm to escort you to the guardhouse."

Mary gasped. He grinned at her. She threw the tape measure at him, which he caught, strung around his neck, and lolled there, as if hanged. She laughed until tears ran. He helped her to her feet and grabbed her in a bear hug.

"Resistance is futile! I know all the moves to subjugate nearly anyone except, well, probably you. There you go. Laugh some more, and then seriously, come with me to the guardhouse. I think I can solve your problem."

"Seriously. I get on my coat and follow you to the guardhouse?"

"I never lie about duty, Miss Blue Eye."

He helped her into her coat and waited while she debated a hat. "Too windy," he said. He unwound his yellow muffler and draped it over her hair. "This is better."

The force of the wind made her gasp. He pulled her arm through his so she couldn't blow away, and they struggled across the parade ground to the small stone building on the banks of the Laramie River.

"No one is going to live in Wyoming Territory for long, and it will never become a state," she announced, when she stood, shivering, inside the guardhouse, where the sergeant of the day grinned at her.

"Shall I bring up the prisoner, Sergeant Blade?" the man asked.

"Absolutely."

She gave Rowan such a look that he backed away and held up his hands in a defensive posture. "Miss Blue Eye, whether you believe me or not—and I have never and will never lie to you—Private München is the answer to . . . to . . . Captain Hayes's prayers."

He was right. Enter one Private Heinrich München, a thin, furtive-looking fellow with worried eyes, probably as worried as hers.

"Make a bow to Miss Blue Eye, Private München," Sergeant Blade said.

The little German obliged, clicking his heels together like a Prussian, and nearly toppled from the effort. While the duty sergeant leaned against his desk and tried not to laugh, Sergeant Blade introduced Mary to a drunkard, a scoundrel, and a tailor. "This is Private München. He drinks too much, and this guardhouse is his second home. He is also a tailor of some renown."

"My goodness," Mary said. "*Really*?"

"*Jawohl,* fräulein. You ask. I do."

"Could you cut out pattern pieces for me?"

"Nothing simpler," Private München said. "I do all button holes. My specialty." He bunched his fingertips to his lips and kissed them.

"That will save me hours," Mary said.

"He'll be able to stay up here and work. With proper supervision, of course," Rowan said.

"Of course," she repeated, amazed at her sudden good fortune. She eyed the tailor. "We'll need another pair of shears and dressmaker pins."

"In my locker for foots in the infantry barrack," he said promptly, which made Rowan grin.

Mary looked around the room, which, with four people in it, was hardly spacious enough for cutting out fabric. "Somehow we can make this work, but . . ."

Rowan indicated the closed door, which he opened. "Take a look, Miss Blue Eye, and tell me what you think."

She followed him into the adjoining room, which contained a long, wooden shelf about knee high and wide, and a potbellied stove. "What in the world?"

"The perfect place to cut fabric, although Private München will have a backache from bending over. This sleeping platform can hold four soldiers on guard duty. It will become Private München's cutting board tomorrow."

No one else was in the room. Mary stood on tiptoe and kissed Sergeant Blade's cheek.

He smiled at her. "No bumbling badgers to disturb that industrious little spider, eh?"

"Not one. She can make those dresses." Mary looked out the little window to the parade ground, wishing she still had fabric for her own dress.

"A penny for your thoughts."

"With Private München helping me now, I would have had time to make my own dress, if I still had the material. I would need a miracle."

"Oh, you never know."

# FIFTEEN

PRIVATE MÜNCHEN WAS as good as his word, cutting out each newspaper pattern, giving her tailoring tips, and demonstrating a superior way to make knife pleats. Mary moved the sewing machine into the room adjacent to the duty sergeant's office and sewed in there. When the German tailor tired of cutting fabric, they traded duties.

Beyond the blessing of working with a talented tailor for longer hours, Mary hoped that Sergeant Blade would feel at liberty to drop by, something that could never happen in the Mastersons' quarters, because he had no business there.

To her delight, Rowan stopped in several times a day. He never seemed to mind holding out a skirt to make certain the pleats were even, although he wouldn't wrap it around himself. When she made a mistake and had to rip out a seam, he obligingly did that for her so she could move quickly to another task.

"Did you help your mother sew when you were a boy?" she asked, on the third day of dress production.

"My parents died of typhoid, and I was raised in an orphanage," he told her as he concentrated on the seam. "No brothers or sisters. Just me."

When she was silent, he didn't even look up. "Mary, if your eyes get blurry with tears, you'll run over your fingers when you sew."

"How do you know I'm crying?" she asked, as she sniffed back tears.

He did look up then. "I know you pretty well. You have a soft heart."

"It's no crime," she said and blew her nose.

"Hardly. I think it's charming."

What could she say to that?

Then he stopped coming. Two days passed, and she found herself looking out the window so often that she sewed the wrong side of the material to one of the skirt panels.

Sobered up, Private München was a true Prussian taskmaster. "Fräulein Blue Eye, focus the mind."

She gave him a tragic look, which allowed the man to relax his standards, as far as fabric was concerned.

"Fräulein, he'll be back."

"I don't know who you're talking about," she assured him.

Sergeant Blade returned the following day. Private München was ironing pleats in the duty sergeant's office next door.

Rowan came in quietly and sat in München's chair. There was no overlooking the sorrow in his eyes. Mary stopped treadling and gave him her attention.

"What has happened?" she asked, wondering if she was prying or if he had come to her—whether he knew it or not—for sympathy.

"It's a bad business. The wife of one of my Ree scouts is dying." He hitched the chair closer. "The surgeon doesn't know what to do, but she's losing weight and in pain nearly all the time now. I like Bill Curly and Mathilde, and I've been sitting with them."

"Is there anything I can do?" Mary asked.

"Not really. I guess I don't care much to be sad by myself."

She thought of the longhouse back home, when families used to all live together and bear one another's burdens. She remembered sitting with other cousins, aunts, and uncles, bored and tired, but aware even as a child that families drew together in times of grief.

The sergeant seemed to take heart as Mary told him about the longhouses and the smokes, sweats, chants, and tears. "I used to think it was alien somehow, since we lived in a modern house with wood floors and hinged doors," she said.

"You don't think it is alien now?"

She shook her head.

"What changed?"

"I did." She said it softly, as if trying out the words. She found them to her liking and repeated them. "I did. I want to go home."

He sighed at that, which told her heart

more than words could have. She glanced at the locket watch pinned to her shirtwaist. Her back ached from doing close work, and the afternoon light was fading fast. She knew she should be heading back to the Masterson quarters soon to hear Victoria's complaints about everything, but she didn't want to.

"Let me go with you to your scout's house. Maybe I can help."

"It's pretty humble," he said.

"Why would that bother me?"

"Let me get your coat."

He insisted on holding her hand as they crossed the footbridge over the Laramie that separated Suds Row from the main garrison. "It's icy," he said, although she couldn't see any ice.

Her arm crooked through his now, he took her past the attached quarters for the families of sergeants and corporals down a trail that led to another attached row, this one for scouts. Beyond that, she saw ragged tipis and wondered if the Laramie Loafers existed there.

"I don't even know what a Ree is," she

said to Rowan as they hurried along, night coming fast.

"Arikara. They hate the Sioux with a great loathing and make excellent scouts, among those Bill Curly. His wife is Mathilde, the daughter of a French trapper and—I think you'll like this—an eastern Indian."

"Oh, I do," she said. "Children?"

"Three girls."

He tapped on the door of the house on the end, then opened it and ushered her in.

To feel shy would have been a waste of time, as three little girls, all tidy with hair in neat braids, swarmed over the sergeant. He picked up the smallest and tickled her, which made her giggle and lean into his chest.

*I love this man*, Mary thought suddenly as she watched him. *I do not want to live without him*. She looked around, hoping she hadn't spoken out loud, and found herself regarded by a thin woman propped up with pillows. The woman gestured to her, and Mary sat beside her bed.

She introduced herself, remembering how her papa taught her. "I am Mary Blue Eye of the Genesee Valley Seneca, Keepers of the Western Door."

To her surprise, the woman nodded. "Sarge has told us about you. I am Mathilde Frere of the Oneida."

"My goodness, we are nearly neighbors!" Mary exclaimed.

"Years have passed since I have been in the land of Ontario," Mathilde said. Her tired eyes took on a wistful look. "Is it as beautiful as ever? Not so much wind? Green in summer?"

"Yes, yes, and yes," Mary said, which made Mathilde laugh and hold her stomach. Mary leaned closer. "People here have no idea, do they?"

Mathilde's eyes brightened. "*We* know. May I call you sister?"

Mary nodded. She understood Indian relationships.

"Hold my hand, and I will close my eyes."

Mary did as Mathilde asked. She looked around the single room, with three small rolls of bedding against one wall, a dish cabinet made of what looked like an apple crate, and a table and stools. Everything was in its place.

"Lean closer."

Mary obeyed.

"My man is going to ask your man to build me a coffin. Sarge will find it hard."

How calm she was. Mary felt tears gather and spill onto her cheeks, quietly, quietly, because that was the Seneca way. She looked at Mathilde and knew it was the Oneida way, too.

"You are far from home, Mathilde," she managed, after monumental effort.

The dying woman shook her head. "Home is here with my man and my children," she whispered. "You will understand someday. You are still young."

*Not as young as I was*, Mary thought, touched to the depths of her soul. She glanced at the little girls, who sat close together on the floor while the oldest one handed around what looked like jerky. Beyond them sat the scout and the sergeant, the scout's hand on the sergeant's back. As she watched, Rowan nodded, then leaned back, as if trying to distance himself from what she knew he must have just agreed to do.

She returned her gaze to Mathilde, then

wiped the woman's face with the damp cloth on the nearby table. She wiped around Indian eyes much like hers and hair wispy now but probably once as full and dark as her own. Disease was exacting a cruel toll, but Mary saw no complaint. She thought of uncomplaining, patient Spider, undefeated by Badger.

"Your mother trained you, too," she whispered and received a tiny smile in answer. *So did mine*, Mary thought. *I must thank her when I see her in a few months.*

The men stood up. "Go now," Mathilde said.

Mary rose, but Mathilde did not release her hand. "One thing."

She sat again and leaned close.

"If you have a picture of your valley, could I borrow it?"

"Sergeant Blade will bring it back tonight."

They left the house hand in hand, with no pretense about ice or snow. "I'm going to build a coffin," Rowan said after they crossed the footbridge. "God help me, but life is hard."

His arm went around her. She hesitated, then put her arm around his waist.

"Walk me home," she said. "I don't want to go there because the lieutenant and Victoria are either really silent or they are carping at each other. It's not a good place now, and I don't like it."

"I wish you had a choice."

"Come inside with me, please. I promised Mathilde a picture of home."

The lieutenant and Victoria were sitting on opposite sides of the postage-stamp parlor in stony silence. Sergeant Blade saluted, and his superior raised a languid finger to his forehead in return.

"I'll only be here a moment, sir," he said.

Mary felt her stomach ache. They must have interrupted them in mid-quarrel. She hurriedly took her favorite painting of the Genesee Valley off the wall in her room. Mama had insisted she take it with her. "So you don't forget us," Mama had said.

She thought of Mathilde so far from her green heaven in Ontario above the border, the white man's line that separated one country from another, when every Indian in the area knew that drawing a line meant nothing. Ah, well.

She handed the small painting to Rowan, who ushered her out the door with him.

The porch was cold and windy, but far better than the parlor, where Mary suspected a brand-new marriage was coming apart.

"Tell Mathilde she can keep it as long as she needs it," Mary said. "What will you line the coffin with?"

"The quartermaster clerk said there is plenty of bed ticking. I'll try to stop by to see you at the guardhouse, but I fear I must hurry with a coffin."

"I'm on schedule now, thanks to your German tailor," she said, walking him down the porch steps, loath for him to leave her.

"I would like to have taken you to the calico ball," he said.

She nearly said, *There will be other dances*, but there wouldn't be, not if she was returning to New York. She gave the darkness overhead a quick glance, looking for wisdom or courage or maybe both, but there were only stars and a rising moon.

"I would have gone gladly," she said, "even in this work dress."

He started to say something, then closed

his mouth. She touched his arm and hurried inside, only because her feet were cold and there was more web to spin.

# SIXTEEN

THERE WAS NO question now that Mary would finish the dresses on time. Private München mentioned that he could do more if she needed to be about her duties in the Masterson household. She assured him that Victoria Masterson could manage well enough.

It really wasn't true. Victoria complained when Mary returned from the guardhouse that she wasn't paying her to neglect her duties. Mary finally took a page from Sergeant Blade's book and gave her employer the Sergeant Stare.

"You bullied me into making fifteen calico dresses for this stupid ball," she snapped. "The ball is in two days, and after that I will do whatever you need, at least until I leave."

Her former friend burst into ready tears and spilled out her own misery at having to decorate that barn of a commissary warehouse for the ball and round up glass dishes and cups for the desserts, which would probably include pounds and pounds of raisins, and what could they do about that? Snow had stopped any wagon trains from Fort Russell north. At least the hostiles were hunkered down on their reservation to the northeast and no one was going to lose any hair, and she didn't think she and the lieutenant were going to be together much longer.

That last bit of misery popped out before Victoria could close her mouth in time. She put her hand to her mouth, her eyes wide and tearful.

Mary's head ached. She wanted to rush to her tiny room and flop on the bed, yearning for solitude to untangle her own thoughts. At least she was leaving Wyoming without the baggage of a marriage gone wrong, or at least at cross purposes, since one or both of the parties were too childish to apologize and try again. Instead, she held out her arms to Victoria, because under all her own turmoil, Mary was kind.

They cried together, Victoria sobbing because she was still a spoiled, pouty thing with her prettiest years probably already behind her, and Mary because she suddenly did not want to leave without her man, who probably thought, when she came right down to it, that *she* was too childish or maybe even too Seneca. How could she know? He was busy with his usual duties, plus making a coffin, which had to render a man melancholy, at the least. There was no time to talk.

She soldiered on in the morning, because Indians did that as well as troopers. She marched herself to the commissary storehouse and used her own money to buy raisins, which she wrapped in fabric scraps. She watched for the child she had first seen weeks ago, trudging behind her mother to the killing floor for scraps. She gave away her raisins.

The word must have got out, because other dark-haired children came for raisins, which meant more trips to the commissary. She handed out raisins, and sewed dratted dresses, and wished for money to buy better food for little friends cast adrift in that uncertain land where the truly poor existed.

Whether he knew it or not, Private München turned the guardhouse duty room into her haven. On the day when only one dress remained, the rest having been handed over to delighted owners, he produced a doll made of white ticking and stuffed with lint from the hospital steward, who was also German and who liked to share a drink now and then with a fellow German.

"Fräulein, with these scraps, think of the dresses we can make." He set the doll beside her sewing machine. "Do you have yarn for hair?"

She did. Mama had sent her with a skein of black yarn to knit herself some mittens. "I do. I'll get it when I go home for luncheon." She held the doll and imagined other dolls with black yarn hair. She knew three little girls about to lose their mother who might need a small distraction. Four girls, counting the hungry one with raisins on her mind.

Her mistake was mentioning the matter to Victoria when she hurried home for a quick sandwich of nothing much beyond army bread and canned meat of mysterious origin. "We'll have the last dress done at the end of the day. After that, Private München and I are going into the doll business."

Victoria clapped her hands, looking more cheerful than Mary had seen her in a week. "What a delightful notion! We can send all the dolls you can make along with the dresses to poor children in Chicago. Mary, this is wonderful."

She tried to set Victoria straight. "These dolls are staying here. There are Indian children *here* who need our attention."

Victoria wouldn't have it. "All our efforts are for the women and children rendered homeless by the Chicago fire. You promised."

"I promised no such thing," Mary fired back. "I have nearly done my task for you. We are using the scraps for another purpose." She left the house before Victoria had time to finish her next sentence, angry and certain she would get a visit soon from Captain Hayes's wife.

Head down against the wind and snow, Mary crossed the parade ground, desperate to see Sergeant Blade, who had plenty of his own worries and no time for hers. The badgers were starting to circle her lovely web, and she wanted to fight back this time, patience be hanged.

Private München heard her out in silence, shaking his head. "When this last one is done," he said, indicating the half-finished dress, "it's back to the cells for me." He brightened. "Can you drag out this dress while I make more doll bodies?"

"I can and will," she said and started picking out a perfectly straight seam in the skirt.

It was worse than she thought. Exactly one half hour later, Captain and Mrs. Hayes arrived in the duty room. Her heart in her throat, Mary looked up from the next seam she was picking out.

"She is making dolls and doll clothes now for the Indian children here and refuses to consider sending them to Chicago, along with the dresses and money we will raise,"

Gertrude Hayes said, pointing an accusing finger in a most theatrical gesture, as if there were many seamstresses in the tiny room and Mary needed to be singled out.

Mary swallowed. She had never needed to stand up for herself at home, not with big brothers and a respected father who clerked for a judge. She had coasted through her life, pampered, well fed, and happy. She also remembered lessons about silence and quiet tears and standing her ground, if need be. She knew those lessons would never apply to her, until finally, at a fort far west of her ancestral home, they did.

Mrs. Hayes was looking at her husband, a captain with the brevet of major, a Medal of Honor recipient for some remarkable bit of military daring at Antietam, a man used to obedience, respected. "William, what are you going to do?"

Private München slipped next door to the duty sergeant's office, abandoning her, or maybe not. He came back into the duty room at the same time she heard someone else running from the other office.

Captain Hayes cleared his throat. "Miss Blue Eye, the dolls should go to Chicago and the worthy poor."

The little spider prepared to defend her web. "There are worthy poor right here, Captain, if you please," she said. "Mathilde, the wife of your Arikara scout, is dying. Sergeant Blade is making her a coffin, as I am certain you know."

He nodded. "Bill Curly is a good and faithful scout."

"Bill and Mathilde have three daughters. I want to give them comfort with dolls and dresses to play with, something to distract them from the sorrow coming their way soon. There is another little girl who follows her mother to the killing floor for meat scraps and offal. I doubt she has ever had a doll of her own. I am making a doll for her, too. I know there are others."

Mary spoke simply, ignoring Mrs. Hayes. She knew enough about women to know that Mrs. Hayes could easily make her husband's life miserable. He was the leader of his troop, she reasoned, and maybe that would be enough to sway her argument. If not, she would not surrender the dolls without a struggle.

"We're dealing in scraps, sir," she said. "Some ticking and some lint. The yarn is mine. Please, sir."

The outside door to the duty room opened, and Sergeant Blade stood there, breathing hard. He must have run from the quartermaster warehouse where she knew he was making the coffin. He was out of uniform, and his sleeves were rolled up to expose muscled forearms covered with sawdust. Mrs. Hayes sniffed and stepped aside, as much as she could in a small room with too many people and far too much anger.

Captain Hayes looked like a man who had just seen the coming of the Lord. "Sergeant Blade, kindly reason with Miss Blue Eye and let me get to work." That last bit was directed at his wife, who glared back.

Rowan shook his head. "She's in the right, Captain. She was asked—no, told—to make dresses, and she has fulfilled that task. Scraps are scraps. That's all Indians get, so what's the harm done? You and I both know that matters out here will only worsen. I say we leave her alone to her work of charity. Real charity."

Mrs. Hayes narrowed her eyes. "I never thought a sergeant in the US Army would side with . . . with . . ."

"An Indian?" Rowan asked. "Yes, I am on Mary's side. She has done what you demanded, ma'am. Don't ask more than she is willing to give."

"What will she do?" Mrs. Hayes demanded.

"I have no idea," Rowan said with a smile, "but I lay odds on Mary to see that four little ones get dolls with fantastic calico wardrobes."

Apparently Captain Hayes agreed. "There you have it, Gertie," he said. "I am figuring out next year's budget. Unless you want to help me with that, I suggest you go home and leave the tailors to their work."

The door slammed. Captain Hayes grinned at Mary and rubbed his hands together. "It'll be cold as can be in my quarters for a few nights, but what the hell? As you were, Miss Mary Blue Eye. Make those doll clothes. Sergeant, back to work."

He left the room, chuckling to himself, and obviously a husband who knew his wife pretty well. Mary couldn't help but think of Shell and His Pony.

Private München went into the adjoining office, muttering something about checking the flat irons, which gave Sergeant Blade perfect leave to gather Mary close. She wasted not a moment and practically leaped into his arms, shivering with the effort of standing up for herself.

"I hope Captain Hayes won't give you a difficult time, Rowan," she said into the sawdust on his shirt. "Thank you. I was afraid of what I was going to do to that dreadful woman."

"I recall you mentioning something once about the Iroquois League and scalping techniques," he said into her hair.

"Oh, you! I would never do such a nasty deed."

"Kiss me, then, and send me back to work."

She kissed him, pulling him close and pressing her lips softly against his, despite the sawdust. He did smell nicely of pine, and that was no liability. He took the liberty of patting her hip, then apologized, his face red.

"Go to work," she said. "We can settle up later."

"That's one way to put it," he told her. He started whistling before he even closed the door, and the little spider sat down to continue the unbroken web.

# Seventeen

THE LAST DRESS found its way to a grateful sergeant's wife by midmorning the next day. By then, Private München had finished three more doll bodies, down to the black yarn hair, which he neatly sewed into black braids. He left the faces blank because neither of them knew how Sioux, Arikara, and Crow felt about personification. They cut out little dresses until after dark, then plotted tomorrow's strategy.

They decided on simple dresses, held together by two hooks and eyes and a ribbon sash. Mary dashed back to the Mastersons' and returned with four of the lieutenant's handkerchiefs, begged for and given to her by a surprisingly cooperative Victoria. Perhaps word had gotten around that Sergeant Blade was even more formidable than anyone had previously imagined and Mary should be helped, for the good of the garrison. Mary was far too wise to question anyone's motive.

The lawn handkerchiefs turned into nightgowns, on which Mrs. Hayes herself obligingly crocheted scalloped edges. The surgeon's wife found scraps of blue wool uniform fabric and hand sewed cloaks herself, to Mary's amazement.

"Hats would have been nice," Mary told Private München when night came on, "but I promised to help Sergeant Blade."

She went to the quartermaster warehouse to sew the blue-and-white mattress ticking into lining for Mathilde Frere's coffin.

Rowan had scrounged a mattress pad from the post surgeon's supply. He helped her tack the lining down and sat back, his eyes tired, to watch her sew it in place. She glanced over at him a time or two and watched him sleep sitting up.

She finished at midnight. Sergeant Blade walked around the coffin, running his hand over the sanded pine, then making sure the hinges didn't squeak. "I'll paint it early in the morning, and then we'll wait," he said.

She would have gone directly home, but as Rowan walked her by the guardhouse, Mary heard the sound of the treadle louder than usual, which meant someone was pushing down extra hard through stiff fabric. Curious, she dragged herself up the few steps and peeked in the window.

She opened the door to see Private München finishing the last of four bags made of canvas, just the right size for dolls with wardrobes. He looked up with a guilty expression, so she knew better than to ask where or how he had acquired canvas.

"You've been working so hard for me," she said.

"It's cold in the cell," he told her. "This is better."

"I wish I could pay you."

"You have, fräulein."

Rowan walked her home. "Tomorrow's the big day?"

"Yes. Since Mrs. Masterson and Mrs. Hayes have been surprisingly helpful today, I told them I would assist with finishing touches on what I will laughingly call the ballroom."

"They've been stringing Fourth of July bunting today, and the band has been practicing. A person could almost dance to their music now." He chuckled. "The commissary clerk has developed a tic in his eye, but he'll recover."

"I think refreshments will be limited, at best," Mary added. "I wish a supply wagon had been able to get through."

"No one wishes that more than I do."

"You were expecting something?"

"I was, but there might be an advantage to this isolation currently foisted upon us," he said as they walked up the front steps. He put his hands on her shoulders. "It might mean you can't leave as soon as you want to."

Mary looked into his tired eyes and knew they mirrored her own. She rested her cheek against his chest, and his arms went around her.

"Don't be in such a hurry to leave, Mary," he said.

The day of the calico ball was like the day

before, but with less wind and snow. Mary looked out her small window that was growing increasingly iced over, longing for a place where spring came when it was supposed to, then ushered in a mild, humid summer, the kind that left her cheeks smooth and soft and not peeling and tough from high plains wind.

She missed the little picture she had loaned to Mathilde Frere. Rowan had told her that Bill Curly had hung it right by her bed. He said she looked at it all the time now.

Mary lay in bed, steeling herself to throw back the warm covers and rush into her clothes. Lately she had started dreaming of dresses and dolls and charitable women who chased her around the guardhouse duty room, demanding this and that. And what could she do about that, since she was a spider? Oh, enough. She made the leap from bed, dressed quickly, and laid a fire in the kitchen range.

The little house was starting to smell fragrant with coffee when someone knocked. She hurried to the front door to see Sergeant Blade. She took his arm to pull him inside. He shook his head and pulled back.

"Mathilde died this morning, while I was painting her coffin."

"I'm so sorry," she said, and meant it. Who would take care of her three daughters? She thought Bill Curly was a good man, but what happened when a good man went on detached detail with his troop? What then? So many questions.

"Rowan, take the three dolls. Maybe the girls will want them right now. Leave me the one doll for my own particular urchin."

He smiled at that. "She'll be by for more raisins any day." He touched his hand to his hat brim. "No dance for us tonight?"

"No dress," she reminded him. "I'm truly sorry, because it would have been fun."

The sergeant seemed to take the disappointment in good cheer, which left Mary a little irked, because she was still Mary, after all, and wanted a few more years to mature and improve her character, or so she reasoned.

"A person can plan and plan, and everything still changes," he said. He tugged the collar higher on his overcoat. "On the bright side, a supply wagon from Fort Russell is stuck at Hunton's stage station. With any luck at all, it might be here tomorrow or by the Fourth of July, depending."

"Alas, too late," she said with a laugh. "Mrs. Masterson told me the ladies were wishing for those canned oysters to arrive in time for stew tonight."

She waved him into the cold again, wondering if there would be a funeral, wondering how the little girls would manage without their mother, and wondering why she wasn't so overjoyed at the prospect of leaving. She wanted to go home. Didn't she?

The day passed quickly. As promised, Mary swept the commissary warehouse floor over and over, looking each time for some improvement and seeing little. She quickly hemmed the last remaining yards of her pretty, dark-blue fabric on the Singer still in the duty room. By the time she finished, the hospital steward had drafted two nearly healthy patients to return the sewing machine to the post surgeon's quarters.

She asked the duty sergeant if she could say goodbye to the tailor, only to be informed that Private München had been released to D

Company again. He had left behind four doll hats woven of broom straw and lined with calico. She took the little dainties with a smile. She would wait a few days, then drop the hats off to their new owners, because every lady needs a hat.

She took her ironed material to the commissary warehouse and let Victoria arrange it on the white bedsheet loaned by the medical department. Her employer set the punch bowl on top and pronounced it successful.

"I'd like the fabric square back when the evening is over. I'll take it back to New York as a souvenir of the dress that wasn't and the dance where I didn't," she joked, and Victoria laughed.

Mary strolled home in the gathering twilight. The wind had died down, and the sun was setting in a fury of vivid pinks and purples that softened into lavender before it turned ordinary again. She heard laughter behind her and saw Victoria and her lieutenant walking arm in arm. Maybe there was hope for the Mastersons. It couldn't be easy for a spoiled girl to turn into an army wife overnight. Perhaps things would work out, and fifty years from now in 1921, when the lieutenant was a general and Victoria terrorizing servants in Washington, DC, the Mastersons would look back on their time at Fort Laramie with fondness. Stranger things had likely happened.

# EIGHTEEN

THAT EVENING AFTER a supper of hash and stewed tomatoes, Mary helped Victoria into the light-blue calico dress with the pale-yellow squares, smoothing down the boned basque and admiring Private München's knife pleats and well-turned buttonholes.

"Here is the plan," Victoria said as she put her gold earbobs in place. "At midnight we will retire to a back room and take off our calico dresses, then put on our ball gowns. Everything will be packed away and ready to mail to the First Congregational Church on Hamlin Avenue. Mrs. Stanley says we have already collected seventy-five dollars for the deserving poor."

Mary nodded. Maybe in a few days or

weeks, or until she left, she could suggest that Victoria and the other officers' wives consider the deserving poor closer to Fort Laramie, across the footbridge and down a draw behind Suds Row.

After the Mastersons left, Mary stood at the window and watched the snow. She hoped that His Pony, Shell, and Smooth Stone were at the Whetstone Creek Agency with Spotted Tail. Rowan had said the newly formed agencies near the Black Hills were protected.

"Let's just hope no one discovers gold in the Black Hills. I hate to think what will happen then," the sergeant had told her last night, when she was tacking down the coffin lining.

"I can tell you what will happen, if someone wants Indian land," she told her reflection in the window glass. "Take care of your family, His Pony."

She had gone to her room to find some stationery for a long letter home to Mama when she heard footsteps on the porch, Rowan Blade footsteps. She knew them by now. Heavens, but the man was persistent. She didn't have a dress.

She opened the door with a smile to see a man with a heavy heart. He carried a pasteboard box, which looked remarkably like something a dressmaker would use. She ushered him inside, and he set the box on the dining room table. *Sukey's Dresses* was stenciled on the box in a flowery script. She looked at the sergeant in surprise.

"The supply train got through a half hour ago. Open it."

She lifted the lid and gasped. It was the dark-blue calico with the white pinpoint dots that Sergeant Blade had picked out for her in Cheyenne, done up with lovely mother-of-pearl buttons and row on row of tucks on the bodice, the work of hours. The shirt had a knee-deep flounce that would look magical on a dance floor.

She ran her hand over the fabric. "Rowan, my goodness." She felt brave and put her arms around his neck. "You did this when you went back to Fort Russell, didn't you?"

"Guilty as charged. I did have paperwork at the fort, and there was time. Sukey didn't mind getting up early to help me out."

He hugged her close, then held her off so

he could look into her eyes. "There's something else, Mary, and it's more important. Sit down."

He didn't look like a man ready to take a lady to a calico ball, even though he wore his uniform. She could almost smell the sorrow under a layer of bay rum. This was a sergeant whose first concern would always be his men.

"What's the matter?" she asked.

"I don't even know how to ask this," he said simply. "I wanted to surprise you with this dress."

"You certainly did," she assured him. "But that's not what is bothering you."

"No. I finished painting Mathilde's coffin by noon. We took it down to Bill Curly an hour ago." He swallowed and shook his head.

He couldn't talk. Mary understood this sort of silence. She thought of her one visit to the Curly quarters, tidy and clean but absolutely bare bones. The girls were dressed neatly, but she doubted they had anything more. She thought of their mother. Her heart went out to this lovely man because she knew what he was asking for without the strength to ask.

She took the dress out and held it against her body. It was complete and utter perfection, the work of a talented dressmaker. She knew it would fit her. She also knew it would fit Mathilde Frere.

Mary held the dress a moment longer, then arranged it back in the box. She put on the lid. "Take it to Mathilde."

He clung to her and cried, and she held him close, smoothing his hair, knowing this man could never do enough for those he led. If by some miracle he asked her to marry him, she would probably have to make allowances for his strong sense of duty. A wife could get used to that, if she loved her husband enough.

He pulled back finally and opened his mouth. She put her fingers to his lips. "Don't you dare apologize to me," she told him, startled at how fierce she sounded, almost like Grandmama Jane in the longhouse when she spoke of soldiers, and longhouses on fire, and retreat.

"Thank you from the bottom of my heart." Rowan picked up the box and left as quietly as he had come.

She sat at the table and stared at her

hands, thinking of all the sorrow in the hut behind Suds Row. Maybe the dolls would help Mathilde's daughters. She knew she would go there tomorrow and take raisins and her love. Maybe the Arikara sat in silence by coffins. She had done that before, impatient and bored. Now she would do it quietly, her heart invested in lives closer to hers than she could have imagined only weeks ago.

How odd to realize that this six-month exile to the Wild West she had undertaken so grudgingly had come full circle and taught her lessons she could have learned nowhere else. She could write Mama about that.

She was still staring at the blank sheet of paper in front of her when she heard Rowan on the porch again, stamping snow off his boots. She rose to open the door, but he opened it before she stood completely on her feet.

He carried a pasteboard box with *Sukey's Dresses* stenciled on the top. She wondered why he hadn't just left the box at the Curly house. Boxes always had their uses.

He set the box on the table and took off his overcoat this time, as if he planned to stay awhile. She went to take his coat from him as a good hostess would, but he tossed it onto the settee.

"Open it."

She smiled at him. "I did, remember? I do hope Bill Curly was all right with what we did."

"He was so appreciative. So were the other scouts' wives. Open it."

"You're a knothead."

He put cold hands on her neck, and she swatted him. "Mary Blue Eye, open it."

She did as he commanded, then stepped back in amazement.

"I asked Sukey to make another dress for you. I picked out this material too. I know wedding dresses aren't supposed to be wool and deep pink, but it's cold here, and I like it."

Mary reminded herself to breathe. The wool was cashmere, softer to the touch than a rose petal and about the same shade. More mother-of-pearl buttons marched down the nicely boned bodice that came to a vee. There was a flounce on this skirt, too.

She picked it up as she had picked up Mathilde's calico dress, holding it to her, smoothing around her curves, which made her smile when the sergeant sighed. Her shoes barely peeked out from below the flounce. She would be the most beautiful bride in this entire godforsaken territory.

"What do you think?"

What did she think? "Do you mean about the dress, or what might have been a proposal, or about needing wool because it's cold outside? Explain yourself, Sergeant Blade."

He took the dress from her and set it carefully on the table. "I've never proposed before. I know that I love you. That's the first thing. I think you will be a lovely mother to our children. Heavens, don't cry about that! They'll probably drive you to distraction on a regular basis."

"I like children," she wailed, and he gave her his handkerchief. "I love you."

"This is encouraging," he teased, more sure of himself now. "If you think the army won't do, I'm one step ahead. That paperwork at Fort Russell was to inform my regimental commanding officer that I will not pursue another enlistment."

"My goodness."

Somehow she was sitting on his lap now, her head tucked against his chest. She wondered what her parents would think of all this. They had always been such careful parents, warning her, teaching her, training her, whether she knew it or not. And here she was sitting on a man's lap and enjoying every second of it.

"How do you plan to support me and all our children?" she asked, which made him laugh and run his hand down her sleeve.

"I build things. Cheyenne needs builders. Maybe your Genesee Valley needs builders. There are any number of pretty towns in Nebraska that need builders, because this country is growing. We can reconnoiter the terrain when we go to New York in a month to get married."

"We're getting married here before we take that trip," she informed this man who might or might not have proposed yet. "Imagine how much fun a Pullman compartment will be if we're married. Um, *have* you proposed yet?"

When he stopped laughing, Sergeant

Blade held her off so he could see her face. "Miss Blue Eye, I love you. The thought of continuing on this arduous journey through life without you is distressing in the extreme. Please marry me. There. Will that do?"

"I will marry you, Sergeant Blade," she said, and kissed him. "You would even move to the Genesee Valley if I wanted you to?"

"The matter is open for consideration. I will live where you are happiest."

She thought of something Mathilde Frere had said. "I will be happiest where you are."

He reached into an inside pocket and took out a blue bead. His fingers were warm now, and she didn't mind them on her neck this time as he tugged out the medicine bag that Shell had given her. He opened the pouch and dropped in the bead next to the brass button and the elk tooth.

"Bill Curly gave me this bead for you." He reached in his pocket again and pulled out a wedding ring. "This is from me. Let's keep it here until we do the deed. I was a busy boy in Cheyenne that morning."

She gasped and hugged him close.

"Rowan, what time do stores open in Cheyenne?"

"Anytime you want, if you bang on the door hard enough." He held her in a loose embrace and fingered her sleeve. "We can go to that blamed calico ball, you know. They're still dancing in the storehouse."

"I'd rather sit here with you," she said, then sat up. "Hmm. There's no church here, and no pastor."

"True." He kissed her cheek, then found her lips. After a lengthy pause he resumed his commentary, out of breath now, but game. "I happen to know of a corporal in D Company, Ninth Infantry, who is an ordained Methodist minister."

"What is he doing in the army?"

Rowan shrugged. "You'd be surprised why men enlist. I don't prod too much, and you shouldn't either."

She digested that. "I'm still a Keeper of the Western Door. I would die if people slighted you because of me."

"That will never happen, Mary Blue Eye. If you haven't already noticed, I'm very good at taking care of my own."

Mary rested her head against his chest. She thought of packing dresses for shipment to the General Relief Committee in Chicago, attending a funeral, finding that little girl who needed more raisins and a doll of her own, and assuring Victoria Masterson that she could manage without a servant.

"I am, too, Sergeant Blade."

What to say about Carla? The old girl's been in the writing game for mumble-mumble years. She started out with short stories that got longer and longer until— poof!— one of them turned into a novel. (It wasn't quite that simple.) She still enjoys writing short stories, one of which is before you now. Carla writes for Harlequin Historical, Camel Press, and Cedar Fort. Her books are found in at least 14 languages.

Along the way, Carla's books and stories have earned a couple of Spur Awards from Western

Writers of America for Short Fiction, a couple of Rita Awards from Romance Writers of America for Best Regency, and a couple of Whitney Awards. Carla lives in Idaho Falls, Idaho, and continues to write, because her gig is historical fiction, and that never gets old.

Follow Carla on Facebook: Carla Kelly
Visit Carla's Website:
www.CarlaKellyAuthor.com

www.ingramcontent.com/pod-product-compliance
Lightning Source LLC
LaVergne TN
LVHW011139050925
820366LV00027B/619